GANDHI
AND
BHAGAT SINGH

V.N. Datta is a professor emeritus of modern history at Kurukshetra University. He was the general president of the Indian History Congress, the resident fellow of Fitzwilliam College, Cambridge (1998), and visiting professor to a number of universities including Moscow, Leningrad and Berlin. Among his much acclaimed publications are *Jallianwala Bagh* (translated into Hindi and Punjabi), *New Light on Punjab Disturbances*, Vol I and II, *Sati: A Historical, Social, and Philosophical Enquiry into the Hindu Rite of Widow-Burning* and *Maulana Azad*. He has contributed articles regularly to journals and the popular press. He is now writing a book called *Ghalib's Dilli (1857)*.

GANDHI
AND
BHAGAT SINGH

V. N. DATTA

RUPA

Published by
Rupa Publications India Pvt. Ltd 2013
7/16, Ansari Road, Daryaganj
New Delhi 110002

Sales centres:
Bengaluru Chennai
Hyderabad Jaipur Kathmandu
Kolkata Mumbai Prayagraj

Copyright © V.N. Datta 2008

First published in hardcover in 2008

All rights reserved.
No part of this publication may be reproduced, transmitted, or
stored in a retrieval system, in any form or by any means, electronic,
mechanical, photocopying, recording or otherwise, without
the prior permission of the publisher.

P-ISBN: 978-81-291-2963-5
E-ISBN: 978-81-291-2632-0

Sixth impression 2025

10 9 8 7 6

The moral right of the author has been asserted.

Typeset by Mindways Design, New Delhi

Printed in India

This book is sold subject to the condition that it shall not, by way
of trade or otherwise, be lent, resold, hired out, or otherwise circulated,
without the publisher's prior consent, in any form of binding or cover
other than that in which it is published.

Twenty days before he was hanged in Central Jail, Lahore on 23 March 1931, Bhagat Singh, then twenty-three years, quoted the following Urdu verse to his younger brother Kultar Singh:

Khush raho ahle watan hum to safar karte hain

Farewell, my countrymen, we are at journey's end.

WAJID ALI SHAH

Contents

Chronological Table — ix
Preface — xiii
Acknowledgements — xvii

1. A Debate on Gandhi's Role — 1
2. Bhagat Singh's Self-Education — 15
3. Gandhi's Attitude — 31
4. Irwin's Action — 56
5. The Trial — 69
6. Karachi Congress — 82
7. Conclusion — 92
8. Recollections — 101

Appendices — 105
Bibliography — 115
Index — 121

Chronological Table

1907	Birth of Bhagat Singh.
1918, May	Joined D.A.V. School, Lahore.
1921	Left D.A.V. School before completing his matriculation examination. Joined National College, Lahore.
1924	Left National College, being pressed by parents to marry. Went to Kanpur and joined Ganeshshankar Vidyarathi's paper, *Pratap* as Balwant. Taught at the National School in Shadipur village, District Aligarh (UP). Attended the Congress session at Belgam.
1925	Returned to Lahore on his grandmother's illness. Warrants issued against him in connection with the Akali Jatha reception accorded during the Jaitu Morcha. Worked for *Arjun*, published from Delhi. Returned to Punjab, worked for *Akali*, an Urdu paper published from Amritsar, also wrote articles for *Kirti*, a Punjabi journal, advocating the cause of workers and peasants.
9 August	Kakori incident in which the ten revolutionaries under the overall command of Ramprasad Bismal absconded with Rs 4,679.

1926	Founded the Naujawan Bharat Sabha with others. Worked as its general secretary.
1927	Implicated in connection with the Dussehra bomb outrage. Falsely, arrested and released on a security bond of Rs 60,000.
1928	Organised the Lahore Students Union, attended the meeting of the Hindustan Republican Association (HRA) at Ferozeshah Kotla ground, Delhi; the HRA renamed as the Hindustan Socialist Republican Association (HSRA) at Bhagat Singh's suggestion.
30 October	Lala Lajpat Rai assaulted by lathi charge while leading the anti-Simon procession at Lahore.
17 November	Lala Lajpat Rai dies.
17 December	Took part in the murder of Assistant Superintendent of Police J.P. Saunders near the police headquarters, Lahore at 4 pm, Escaped to Calcutta.
1929, 8 April	Two bombs and leaflets thrown into the Central Assembly Delhi at 12.30 pm, courted arrest with B.K. Dutt.
7 May	Trial on the Assembly Bomb Case began in the Court of the Additional District Magistrate F.B. Pool.
6 June	Statement made before the Sessions Judge Leonard Middleton when regular trial began.
12 June	Judgement pronounced on the Assembly Case, and sentenced to transportation for life.
15 June	Hunger strike for better facilities in Delhi jail.
10 July	Trial in the Lahore Conspiracy Case before the special Magistrate R.S. Krishan.
13 September	Jatindra Nath Das died after sixty-three days of hunger strike.

1930, 1 May	A Special Tribunal was set up under the Lahore Conspiracy Ordinance to try the culprits involved in the case.
20 June	The Tribunal reconstituted.
7 October	Judgement in the Lahore Conspiracy Case pronounced. Death sentence awarded.
1931	Defence Counsel submitted a petition to the Privy Council which was rejected on 27 February.
23 March	Hanged in Lahore Central Jail at 7.30 pm.

Preface

This work is a revised and enlarged version of the keynote address delivered at the International conference held on 'Bhagat Singh and His Times' at the ICCSR complex in Punjab University, Chandigarh, from 27 to 30 September 2007. The conference was organised under the auspices of the Indian Council of Historical Research and the Institute of Punjab Studies.

This year marks the birth centenary of Bhagat Singh and the seventy-fifth year of his execution. Bhagat Singh was hanged in the Central Jail in Lahore on 23 March 1931 at 7.30 pm. A number of books have been published in 2007 relating to his role in the national movement. His own writings and what his contemporaries and others wrote on him have also been published. The present study belongs to a different category—it focuses on a single issue: Mahatma Gandhi's attitude to Bhagat Singh's trial and execution. Most historical narratives discuss or refer to Gandhi's reactions on Bhagat Singh's trial and execution. When Bhagat Singh and his comrades were tried and hanged, Gandhi by then had emerged as the most influential political leader with a mass following in the country. He was loved and respected for his moral integrity and practical sagacity.

Historians give different explanations about Gandhi's attitude to the trial and execution of Bhagat Singh. Some writers allege that Gandhi was not emotionally involved in saving Bhagat Singh's life from the gallows because of his obsession with his creed of non-violence and his repudiation of violent means, which Bhagat Singh had adopted for the fulfilment of his plans to wreck British power in India. Other writers argue that Gandhi did make desperate efforts to save Bhagat Singh's life till the end; and he failed not for want of efforts on his part but he failed because the power to commute Bhagat Singh's death sentence lay not in his hands, but in the Viceroy Irwin's. These writers assert that Gandhi had put the maximum pressure on Irwin to commute Bhagat Singh's death sentence, but the Viceroy duped him by giving him false hopes.

A general assumption in the works published so far is that the issue of the commutation of Bhagat Singh's death sentence was the one that could have been amicably resolved between Gandhi and Irwin with tact and compassion. The assumption is questionable. This study argues that the question of Bhagat Singh's life and death has to be seen from a broader perspective, especially within the framework of the British Imperial system operating in the country, which is generally ignored.

Secondly, some of the historians in the country are of the view that Bhagat Singh was a convinced and confirmed Marxist, Socialist and Leninite. Such a one-dimensional view ignores, obscures and undermines the other tangible influences which formed his social and political outlook. Bhagat Singh grew and evolved himself by drawing inspiration from several quarters. He also meditated on his own experiences. This work traces the growth and evolution of his thinking through various stages of his development by identifying the influences that worked on him.

Undeniably Bhagat Singh by his sacrifices had aroused national consciousness in the country. The question is what was his legacy? What was his achievement? These are uncomfortable questions to answer. This study shows that Bhagat Singh and his associates were as much the victims of British imperialism as of Gandhian politics. In the late Twenties and early Thirties of the last century, Gandhi regarded Bhagat Singh's mode of militant nationalism, and the extreme left-wing political activity as the most injurious to the cause of Indian independence. As a strategist he appropriated the positive features of both the approaches and made them with some modifications an integral part of the Congress policy and programme, which he presented later at the Congress session at Karachi, about a week after Bhagat Singh's execution.

From contemporary evidence, especially from the Lahore Conspiracy Case trial proceedings, it is evident that Sukhdev was the real brain and organiser of the entire programme, plans and activities of the militant nationalists of the period, but his role has been ignored. As a silent worker, operating in the background, he shunned the limelight. Sukhdev still awaits a historian!

V.N. Datta
New Delhi

Acknowledgements

In the interpretation of this work, I am grateful to Ainslie T. Embree, Bipan Chandra, Sabyasachi Bhattacharya, T.R. Sareen and Chaman Lal for reading the first draft of this study. Their comments have been encouraging and I have tried to incorporate some of their suggestions in my text. I thank Kuldip Nayar, the biographer of Bhagat Singh, who has clarified, with his usual candour, some questions relating to Bhagat Singh's trial. I am grateful to Anil Nauriya for his advice and guidance. His scholarly articles on 'Gandhi and Singh' opened up a lively debate on Gandhi and his attitude to Bhagat Singh's execution. R.S. Bawa has clarified some of the points regarding the functioning of the police system during the British rule for which I offer my thanks. I also thank Inder Malhotra for giving me useful information about the key witness in Bhagat Singh's trial.

Harish K. Puri's refreshing and meticulous study of the Ghadr movement gave me a new perspective in understanding Bhagat Singh's ideological orientation. For his patience in enlightening me on a number of queries, I offer my special thanks. My former colleague, K.C. Yadav, has published a series of volumes on Bhagat Singh and his activities, which provide a first-class primary source-material. With his knowledge of a vast array of source-material, locating various works and helping out with the references, he has rescued me for making untenable generalisations, for which I express my gratitude. I warmly thank my daughter Nonica, for her advice and support and making this work possible. I have benefited much from my discussions with Nayana Goradia especially with regard to Bhagat Singh's association with the Bengal revolutionaries and I record my appreciation for it. Jehanara Wasi's advice, especially on literary matters, has been invaluable and I thank her.

At the National Archives of India, Jaya Ravindran and Usha Kaul made my task easier for making available to me the material for consultation in the shortest possible time and helping me in several ways to meet my requirements for which I offer my sincere thanks. I also thank the authorities of Nehru Memorial Museum and Library for permitting me to consult the private collections in the Mss-room.

At the India International Centre Library, the library staff, especially Kanchan Nagpal, Surinder, Rajeev Mishra, and Hema assisted me in securing books from various quarters for which I am grateful. I am deeply beholden to Sangeeta Kaul for obtaining the requisite information on academic matters for me in time. I thank Raji Subramanian for her unstinted support in typing this work.

My special thanks go to Trisha Bora for her dedicated editorial support in the revision of this text.

And, finally, for my wife's sustained emotional involvement in this and other literary works which I take up, no acknowledgement can suffice.

1

A Debate on Gandhi's Role

The issue of Mahatma Gandhi's attitude to Bhagat Singh's trial and execution has sparked much controversy among historians and writers. Some writers allege that Gandhi could have saved Bhagat Singh's life if he had wished, but regrettably, he didn't and wouldn't, and his failure in saving Bhagat Singh's life from the gallows leaves a black spot on his political career. On the other hand, Gandhi's own party workers, followers and some writers clarify with pathetic earnestness that Gandhi failed not because of his lack of interest in the well-being of Bhagat Singh, but because of the conditioning circumstances which lay beyond his control. I think that this controversy, which has stimulated much literature on the subject, needs further clarity and understanding. Let us first see how historians and other writers—this is not an enumeration, but an exemplification—view and explain Gandhi's attitude to the trial and execution of Bhagat Singh.

In his biography of Bhagat Singh, Kuldip Nayar holds the view that Gandhi was very concerned about Bhagat Singh, but he did not approve of his violent methods because he thought that such means would do much harm to the country.[1] That is why Gandhi even refused to associate himself with the move to raise a statue in honour of Bhagat Singh's martyrdom.[2] S.R. Bakshi maintains in his study that Gandhi made some effort to save Bhagat Singh's life, but he did not put sufficient pressure on the Viceroy Lord Irwin to commute his life sentence. Bakshi thinks that 'a higher political pressure' would have resolved the issue in favour of the revolutionary youth.[3] But he does not elaborate on the kind of political pressure that would have worked!

In his article 'Bhagat Singh, Bose and the Mahatma', Ashok Celly castigates Gandhi for not rescuing Bhagat Singh from his execution because of 'his pathological dislike or fear of revolution' and his commitment to non-violence.[4] To emphasise Gandhi's indifference to the fate of Bhagat Singh, Celly recalls how the Mahatma had thrown out the star politician Subhas Chandra Bose from the Congress because of his ideological differences with him even though he was a democratically elected Congress president.[5]

In his biography of Bhagat Singh, D.S. Deol regrets that Gandhi did not make the issue of Bhagat Singh's execution a precondition of his settlement with the Viceroy because he felt that it was not in the larger interests of his country. In support of his contention, Deol quotes from Gandhi's article in *Young India*, 'I might have made the commutation a term of the settlement—it could not be made. The Working Committee agreed with me in not making commutation of Bhagat Singh's death sentence a condition precedent to truce. I could therefore only mention it.'[6] Deol emphasises that 'a leader could hardly be expected to secure the commutation of the death sentence of Bhagat Singh' and writes, 'If the boys should be hanged they had better be hanged before the Congress session (Karachi) than after it.'[7] General Mohan Singh of INA fame, too, like Deol took a similar view when he wrote, 'But Gandhi could not rise above the false prestige of his philosophy of non-violence because Bhagat Singh's release would have given strength to a group of revolutionary heroes which Gandhi could not tolerate.'[8]

In his book on Bhagat Singh, K.K. Khullar defended Gandhi and appreciated his role in trying to save Bhagat Singh. Khullar argued that the Viceroy proved more clever, and duped Gandhi in believing that he was in sympathy and was also doing his best in the matter.[9] S. Gopal in his study of the viceroyalty of Lord Irwin, skirts the question of Bhagat Singh's reprieve and execution. He writes that 'it speaks for the integrity of these men (Gandhi and Irwin) that in the circumstances they felt that it would be dishonest to postpone the execution of Bhagat Singh till the Congress session is over'.[10] S. Gopal does not discuss the question of Bhagat Singh's commutation of death sentence. On the other hand, he considers Irwin's policy as 'overwhelmingly right' to an extent that he did more than 'any men of his own time to keep alive the faith of the two people (Gandhi and Irwin) in each other'.[11]

Quoting from Gandhi's speech, which he had delivered at a mass meeting in Delhi on 7 March 1931, that 'those who use the sword will perish by the sword', D.G. Tendulkar argues that Gandhi's moral commitment to non-violence prevented him from supporting Bhagat Singh's acts of violence, and whatever he said in his favour was motivated by his desire to appease the extremists who were critical of the Congress' indifference to saving his life.[12] Pattabhi Sitaramayya, the official Congress historian, gives an account of the Gandhi-Irwin talks about Bhagat Singh's death sentence. According to Sitaramayya, the Viceroy was reserved about Bhagat Singh's death sentence, and 'never made any promise beyond assuring that he would employ his good offices with the Punjab government in this,...Anyway, Lord Irwin was unable to help in the matter'.[13]

And of Gandhi's attitude, Sitaramayya writes:

> That Gandhi himself definitely stated to the Viceroy that if the boys should be hanged, they had better be hanged before the Congress, than after. There would be no false hopes lingering in the breasts of the people. The Gandhi-Irwin Pact would stand or fall on its own merits of the Congress, and on the added fact that the three boys had been executed.[14]

Basing his account largely on D.P. Das's essay in the *Mainstream* (Independence Day issue, 1970, 14-16) Manmathnath Gupta in his book entitled *What Gandhi Did and Did Not Do* accuses Gandhi of practising chicanery and acting in a double-faced manner, professing sympathy for Bhagat Singh in public, but in secret, settling with the Viceroy a suitable time for his execution. Gupta argues that Gandhi was 'not emotionally involved' in saving Bhagat Singh's life, because he did not want his Pact with the Viceroy to be wrecked.[15] Gupta also points out that the public commendation of Bhagat Singh's heroic spirit was causing much worry to the Mahatma, who regarded such manifestation of feelings as a sign of sheer political immaturity.

Generally, the British historians tend to ignore the Bhagat Singh case. Percival Spear, C.H. Philips and Judith Brown are silent on the subject. Sir Penderel Moon in his study of British rule, wrote that in the case of Bhagat Singh's reprieve, Irwin refused to be moved by political considerations.[16] Roy Jenkins, a perceptive analyst of Irwin's administration wrote that the Viceroy had to appease the official opinion to execute Bhagat Singh.[17] Irwin's biographer, Allan Comphell Johnson noted that both Gandhi and Irwin, who greatly valued the sanctity of human life, discussed whether Bhagat Singh's life should be spared or not, and arrived at a decision. Johnson wrote:

> Sir Herbert Emerson, the Home Member, who was called upon to play a prominent role in Delhi negotiations records listening with amazement to Irwin and Gandhi after agreement had been reached by them that Bhagat Singh must be executed, engaged in a prolonged decision not as between two statesmen but as between two saints on the sanctity of human life.[18]

Andrew Roberts, a distinguished biographer of Irwin's life, wrote that after Gandhi's appeal to him to commute Bhagat Singh's death sentence, 'Irwin spent a sleepless night with his conscience. The next day he refused to commute the death sentence and he and his comrades were hanged.'[19] Gandhi had pleaded what a good effect his reprieve would have, but the Viceroy turned it down.

In Chapter fourteen 'Gandhi's Truth' of his book *The Trial of Bhagat Singh*, A.G. Noorani maintains that Gandhi's efforts in saving Bhagat Singh's life were half-hearted because of his failure to make a strenuous appeal to the Viceroy for the commutation of his death sentence to life.[20] To emphasise his indifference to the fate of Bhagat Singh, Noorani writes that Gandhi did not care to see Bhagat Singh when he was on hunger strike in jail. Noorani asserts that during his conversations with the Viceroy, Gandhi pleaded not for the commutation of Bhagat Singh's death sentence, but for its suspension. He argues further:

> Gandhi could have intervened effectively to save Bhagat Singh. He did not till the last. Later claims such as that 'I brought all the pressure at my command on him' (the Viceroy) are belied by researches that came to light later. In this tragic episode Gandhi was not candid, neither to the nation or even to his closest colleagues about the talks with the Viceroy, Lord Irwin in saving Bhagat Singh.[21]

Noorani claims that Gandhi in his negotiations with the Viceroy did not take his colleagues into confidence. According to Noorani, Gandhi was more interested in saving his Pact with the Viceroy than care for the one, who fired by patriotic spirit, was ready to die for the love of his country.

Gandhi's attitude to Bhagat Singh's life sentence and execution has been discussed and debated in a series of articles published in the *Mainstream* weekly. The participants in these lively and animated debates are non-professional historians, which indicates a healthy sign for the growth of historical knowledge. Controversies on historical themes tend to enrich the quality of historical thought. The *Mainstream* debate also shows how the memory of the legendary Bhagat Singh continues to evoke interest in the public mind even now.

The starting point of the debate in the *Mainstream* was the publication of D.P. Das's article 'Gandhi and Bhagat Singh' in 1970.[22] Basing his study on Irwin's biographies, and the Irwin-Gandhi correspondence, Das presents Gandhi as a wheeler-dealer who believed that:

> The Delhi Pact was much more important than the lives of one revolutionary or three. Bhagat Singh and his comrades were the tragic cases that arose at the time which almost stood between a settlement with Irwin by Gandhi.[23]

In the concluding part of his essay, Das charges Gandhi with deception for using devious means in his discussions with the Viceroy on the question of Bhagat Singh's death sentence. But Das also mentions that even ancient Hindu scriptures contain several examples of virtuous men like Rama and Yudhishtira who had acted deceptively for the sake of noble objects nullifying his charges against Gandhi.

Contesting A.G. Noorani's views as expounded in his book *The Trial of Bhagat Singh* that Gandhi did not take sufficient interest in saving Bhagat Singh's life, Anil Nauriya asserts that falling short of making the commutation of Bhagat Singh's death sentence a part of his Pact with the Viceroy, Gandhi did whatever he could to put the maximum pressure on the Viceroy not to hang Bhagat Singh.[24] Nauriya emphasises that Gandhi asked not for the suspension of Bhagat Singh's death sentence but its commutation. Nauriya also highlights that Gandhi had sent Sir Tej Bahadur Sapru, M.R. Jayakar and Srinivasa Sastri to the Viceroy to plead for the commutation of Bhagat Singh's death sentence.

Claiming to base his account on the *Diary of Mahadev Desai* (in Gujarati) edited by C.B. Dalal, and other primary source-materials, Nauriya wrote that, 'Evidently Gandhi's involvement in the clemency effort was multi-pronged and more thorough, than Noorani has been able even to visualize.'[25] Nauriya concludes that Gandhi clearly treated the non-execution of Bhagat Singh as a part of the Gandhi-Irwin Pact.[26] In his rejoinder to Nauriya's article (6 April 1996), sticking to his earlier view as discussed in his book, *The Trial of Bhagat Singh*, A.G. Noorani reiterates that on the question of saving Bhagat Singh's life, Gandhi's pleadings were 'manifestly weak'.[27] According to Noorani, Gandhi was more interested in postponing the death sentence than its commutation, the view he shares with D.P. Das. He acknowledges further that Gandhi did make some effort on 31 March 1931, but it was too late, and if he had done so earlier, then there was the chance of saving Bhagat Singh's life. In reply to Noorani's rejoinder, Nauriya in his article 'The Writing of History' reiterates that Gandhi had been making serious efforts since 19 February 1931 to save Bhagat Singh from the gallows, which is evident from the source-material he had used, including Mahadev Desai's diary.[28]

Joining the debate, Prem Basin, a well-known left-wing politician, repudiates D.P. Das's charge that Gandhi was devious and untruthful in his negotiations with the Viceroy.[29]

Agreeing with Nauriya, Basin states that:

Gandhi had succeeded in obtaining a private assurance from the Viceroy that the death sentence would be commuted and Gandhi had conveyed the assurance to the Working Committee. This was meant to be strictly confidential, but a member of the committee hailing from Punjab divulged it to a section of the Press which led to a revolt by the Steel Frame with threats of mass resignations—and Irwin had to bow to their pressure.[30]

Disagreeing with Basin's views that Gandhi had played a positive role in saving Bhagat Singh's life, Noorani in his article 'Gandhi and Bhagat Singh' insists that the records of the Gandhi-Irwin correspondence, which constitute a first-class primary evidence, show clearly that Gandhi was wanting in his efforts to press the Viceroy to commute Bhagat Singh's death sentence.[31]

In a comprehensive article entitled 'Clemency Effort for Bhagat Singh', Nauriya rebuts Noorani's view that Gandhi did little or nothing to obtain clemency for Bhagat Singh.[32] He argues that when Gandhi urged the Viceroy for suspension of Bhagat's Singh's death sentence in his letter dated 23 March 1931, he desired not postponement, but 'suspension in addition to the commutation proposal, and not in exclusion of it'.[33] Nauriya regrets—this is an important point—that the issue of Bhagat Singh's execution has not been examined from the London (the Home government), and Punjab (the Punjab government) angles.[34]

Recently two publications came out on Bhagat Singh, the first by S. Irfan Habib, *To Make the Deaf Hear: Ideology and*

Programme of Bhagat Singh and His Comrades: Three Essays, and the second by Kuldip Nayar, *Without Fear: The Life and Trial of Bhagat Singh*.[35] Habib's comprehensive and lucid study focuses on Bhagat Singh's ideological orientation, which is summed up in Chapter four of his book entitled 'Ideology and Programme of the Hindustan Socialist Republican Association'.[36] His study shows that Gandhi was hostile to Bhagat Singh's use of violence in the realisation of his aims. But on the question whether Gandhi tried to save his life or not, Habib is somewhat nebulous. Of course, Habib emphasises that some of the young Congress leaders, like Jawaharlal Nehru and Subhas Chandra Bose were not only sympathetic, but willing to help Bhagat Singh.

Irfan Habib maintains that Gandhi suggested to the Viceroy Irwin to postpone the execution till the session (Karachi Congress) was over. But Irwin opposed the idea on the ground that postponement was beyond his power. He further said that postponement might lead to false hopes, and he did not wish to be called dishonest by the falsification of hopes.[37] Except this statement, which is of little significance, Habib has nothing to add on Gandhi's interest in saving Bhagat Singh's life. Kuldip Nayar's new book, *Without Fear: The Life and Trial of Bhagat Singh* is a revised and expanded version of his earlier work entitled *The Martyr, Bhagat Singh: Experiments in Revolution*. On Gandhi's attitude towards Bhagat Singh's death sentence, Nayar reiterates his earlier view that Gandhi was concerned about saving his life, which is evident in the Gandhi-Irwin correspondence; but he did not wish to identify himself with the revolutionaries because that would negate his stand.[38]

From the above review of the historical literature produced on Gandhi's attitude to Bhagat Singh's death sentence, three views emerge: firstly, that Gandhi had made serious efforts to save Bhagat Singh's life but he failed because the Viceroy betrayed him by giving him false hopes, and Gandhi fell into his trap. Secondly, it is argued that Gandhi's own commitment to non-violence, and his anxiety to save his Pact with the Viceroy from being wrecked, dampened his enthusiasm to support the commutation of Bhagat Singh's death sentence. Thirdly, it is mentioned by some historians that Gandhi had reached an agreement with the Viceroy on the commutation of Bhagat Singh's death sentence, but this inside information was divulged publicly in a spirit of bravado by a member of the Congress Working Committee. The disclosure of this secret deal triggered off a strong reaction from the British civil servants who threatened to resign if Bhagat Singh's death sentence was commuted. Under such circumstances, the Viceroy felt helpless, and he declined to commute the death sentence.

I think the assumption that Gandhi and Irwin were sovereign shapers of events so stridently bruited is questionable. Things happen differently in the historical realm. Gandhi and Irwin were not the repositories of power because they were working under constraints, which set limits to their actions. The question is whether the Viceroy and Gandhi had the choice, and elbow room for manoeuvre and dexterity of manipulation to decide on their own the question of Bhagat Singh's death sentence. The Kuru King Dhritarashtra and the Pandava Prince Yudhishtira could not call the Mahabharata war off. In 1807 at Tilsit despite their best efforts, the sovereigns Napoleon and

Alexander I brought not peace but a perpetuation of conflicts. However powerful and influential men may be, the system of necessity operates in the vicissitudes of human affairs to limit and circumscribe their mode of conduct. At the same time in the run of events in general, a causally determined process cannot stifle the spontaneity and autonomy of free will.

We have noticed above that there are two opposite views on Gandhi's attitude regarding Bhagat Singh's death sentence. Subjects like this have to be envisaged within a larger framework. There are several questions to answer in regard to Gandhi's attitude towards Bhagat Singh's execution. Was Gandhi interested in saving Bhagat Singh's life? Did he put adequate pressure on the Viceroy and the government for the commutation of Bhagat Singh's death sentence'? Or was Gandhi half-hearted, and a double-crosser, playing a duplicitous role, admiring Bhagat Singh in public for his patriotism, etc., on one hand, and kowtowing to the British government for executing Bhagat Singh on the other.

To understand how in the difficult situation confronting them, Irwin and Gandhi had acted on Bhagat Singh's death sentence, we have to relate Gandhi's negotiations with the Viceroy to his own political ethics and political circumstances of his times, the pressure of Indian and British public opinion, the role of the Viceroy, the working of the British bureaucracy, and imperial system in India and England. Each of these aspects has to be treated separately in our discussion to arrive at our conclusions.

Notes

1. Kuldip Nayar, *The Martyr Bhagat Singh: Experiments in Revolution*, p. 144.
2. Ibid.
3. S.R. Bakshi, 'Gandhi and Bhagat Singh', in *Selected Collections on Bhagat Singh*, M.M. Juneja (ed.), pp. 249-57.
4. Ashok Celly, 'Bhagat Singh, Bose and the Mahatma', in *Mainstream*, 20-26 June 2007, p. 18.
5. Ibid, p. 19.
6. D.S. Deol, *Shaheed Bhagat Singh, A Biography*, p. 85.
7. Ibid.
8. Ibid., p. 86.
9. K.K. Khullar, *Shaheed Bhagat Singh*, p. 80.
10. S. Gopal, *The Viceroyalty of Lord Irwin*, p. 115.
11. Ibid., p. 139.
12. D.G. Tendulkar, *Mahatma, Life of Mohan Das Karamchand Gandhi*, pp. 78-80.
13. Pattabhi B. Sitaramayya, *The History of the Congress*, vol. I, p. 745.
14. Ibid.
15. Manmathnath Gupta, *Bhagat Singh and His Times*, p. 212.
16. Sir Penderel Moon, *The British Conquest and Division of India*, p. 1052.
17. Roy Jenkins, 'A Liberal Viceroy', in *Nine Men of Power*, p. 147.
18. Allan Campbell Johnson, *Viscount Halifax: A Biography*, p. 316.
19. Andrew Roberts, *The Holy Fox, A Biography of Lord Halifax*, p. 41.
20. A.G. Noorani, *The Trial of Bhagat Singh: Politics of Justice*, p. 240.
21. Ibid., p. 252.

22. *Mainstream* (Independence Day issue), 1970, pp. 14-16.
23. Ibid., p. 16.
24. Anil Nauriya, 'Execution of Bhagat Singh: Some Clarifications on Noorani's Narative', in *Mainstream*, 6 April 1996, pp. 27-32.
25. Ibid., p. 31.
26. Ibid., p. 130.
27. A.G. Noorani, 'Gandhi and Bhagat Singh', in *Mainstream*, 20 June 1996, pp. 7-10, see p. 7 in particular.
28. Anil Nauriya, 'The Writing of History', in *Mainstream*, 22 June 1996, pp. 11-12.
29. Prem Basin, 'Bhagat Singh and Gandhi's Truth', in *Mainstream*, 27 July 1996, pp. 19-23, see p. 23.
30. Ibid.
31. A.G. Noorani, 'Gandhi and Bhagat Singh', in *Mainstream*, 7 September 1996, p. 26.
32. Anil Nauriya, 'Clemency effort for Bhagat Singh', in *Mainstream*, 22 March 1997, pp. 17-32.
33. Ibid., p. 18.
34. Ibid., p. 17.
35. S. Irfan Habib, *To Make the Deaf Hear: Ideology and Programme of Bhagat Singh, and His Comrades: Three Essays*, Kuldip Nayar, *Without Fear: The Life and Trial of Bhagat Singh*.
36. Ibid., pp. 105-32.
37. Ibid., p. 83. This account is based on the journal *Mukti*, July 1972, p. 16.
38. Kuldip Nayar, *The Martyr Bhagat Singh: Experiments in Revolution*, pp. 150-53.

2

Bhagat Singh's Self-Education

Bhagat Singh did not learn politics from books. He belonged to the family of staunch nationalists and revolutionaries. His grandfather Sardar Arjun Singh was an active Arya Samaj supporter. His father Sardar Kishan Singh had close associations with Bhai Parmanand who was later sentenced to life imprisonment and dispatched to the Andamans. In fact, both Sardar Kishan Singh and his famous revolutionary brother Ajit Singh lived in Parmanand's house in Lahore. There is reason to believe that Sardar Kishan Singh was aiding the revolutionary organisations (1914-15) financially for which he was interred under the Defence of India Act.[1] He was also the manager of the Hindu Orphanage for sometime. As a sensitive and intelligent youth, Bhagat Singh was a witness to the traumatic events in Punjab which had a profound impact on his mind and moulded his thinking. The political activities of his firebrand uncle Sardar Ajit Singh aroused his curiosity from his childhood, and he made anxious enquiries about his whereabouts from Jawaharlal Nehru, who met him in jail. Ajit Singh had been deported to Mandalay with Lala Lajpat Rai in 1907 by the British government under the infamous Regulation of 1818 for his active participation in the Agrarian Disturbances. Ajit Singh and Lala Lajpat Rai toured Punjab, rallied the support of the peasantry and landowning classes, and launched a campaign for the abolition of the iniquitous Colonisation Bills. Ajit Singh was initially exiled to Burma, but later he escaped to Iran and Turkey and reached Brazil.

Bhagat Singh and his comrades, Batukeshwar Dutt and Jatindranath Das, the accused in the Lahore Conspiracy Case, were on hunger strike when Jawaharlal Nehru met them in Borstal Jail in Lahore on 9 August 1929. They had undertaken a fast in protest to improve the lot of political prisoners, who were treated like convicts.

In his letter to his son Jawaharlal Nehru dated 20 December 1929, Motilal Nehru gives some information about his meeting with Bhagat Singh and his comrades. He had gone to Lahore to supervise the arrangements made for the forthcoming session of the Indian National Congress, when his son was to be elected to its Presidency, Motilal Nehru wrote:

> I went to the Court of the Special Magistrate who is trying the Lahore Conspiracy case this morning. The accused who were all in the dock greeted me with their usual cries: 'Long live the Revolution—Down with Imperialism'. The more prominent members of the group were then introduced to me, the first being Bhagat Singh. They were a jolly lot and were evidently very well looked after. I chatted with some

for some time, and then they assembled round the fire provided in the dock, and sang a moving national song.[2]

Bhagat Singh expressed his desire to meet Motilal Nehru, but he was in a hurry to get back to Delhi, and promised to meet him and his associates later.[3]

Jawaharlal Nehru wrote in his autobiography that he was struck by Bhagat Singh's 'intellectual face, remarkably calm and peaceful'.[4] If the word intellectual means a person whose mind is bubbling with ideas, and who has a specific agenda, and a blueprint for the future, and is engaged in formulating and holding independent views on problems relating to human welfare and determined to implement them, then Bhagat Singh qualifies to be called an intellectual in the authentic sense of the term.

Bhagat Singh's school education remained incomplete. He did join D.A.V. High School, Lahore, and stayed in its boarding house for a year, but had to leave his studies without passing his matriculation test. From his writings in the *Kirti*, it is evident that the revolutionary activities of Madan Lal Dhingra, a resident of Amritsar, belonging to an aristocratic family of Punjab (who had killed Sir Curzon Wyllie in London in 1909) aroused his admiration. In his essay on Dhingra published in the *Kirti*, Bhagat Singh paid a glowing tribute to Dhingra for his love for his motherland, and his sacrifices, which had earned him the glory of martyrdom.[5] Bhagat Singh wrote, 'I have set out his biography. Fearing that in due course of time we might even forget his name, I am placing, whatever facts I could gather about him before the readers.'[6] Bhagat Singh ends his essay with his salutations: 'What a brave man he was.

It is great to remember him. Many salutations to the valuable jewel of the dead country.' The word 'dead' in the sentence is significant as it indicates that according to Bhagat Singh, the year 1928, when he wrote his essay on Dhingra, the country was politically quiescent, needing the quickening of political pace and activity.

It is evident from Bhagat Singh's writings that he kept himself fully informed about the activities of the revolutionaries in Punjab who had sacrificed their lives for the love of their country. The courage and patriotism of the political activists involved in the Delhi Conspiracy Case, especially Bhai Balmukand Chibber, a Mohyal Brahman, (a co-accused), a cousin of the famous revolutionary Bhai Parmanand, greatly impressed him.[7] Balmukand was hanged on 11 May 1915 for throwing a bomb on the Viceory Lord Hardinge in Chandni Chowk, New Delhi on 23 December 1912, and his wife Ram Rakhi starved herself to death later.

Of all the political movements organised for the liberation of the country, Bhagat Singh regarded the Ghadrites as the most suitable model for the liberation of the country. The Ghadrites had tried to follow the methods of the Russian Revolution in their plan of uprooting British authority in India. On 15 November 1913, the Ghadr Party published a weekly paper, *Ghadar* with Har Dyal as its chief editor. On the front page, beneath the name of the paper, was the caption 'Enemy of the British'. Sir Michael O'Dwyer, Lieutenant Governor of Punjab, in Chapter XIII of his autobiography *India As I Knew It* (1885-1925) emphasised how the Ghadrites had made Punjab, by early 1915, the centre of their political activity, and posed as a big challenge to the authority of the government.[8]

Rash Bihari Bose and N.G. Pingley masterminded the programme of the Ghadr Party. The Ghadrites raided arsenals, killed policemen, derailed trains, and committed a number of dacoities in Punjab to spread terror. They even targeted banks to collect funds for the implementation of their revolutionary programme. What chiefly attracted Bhagat Singh was the secular and democratic character of the Ghadr Party, which had made a clear distinction between religion and politics, and never allowed them to mix. Bhagat Singh wrote a short, moving and high-spirited life story of Kartar Singh Sarabha, a youth of eighteen and a half years old, whom he regarded as the main organiser in Punjab.[9] The Ghadr adherents who formed the nucleus of the new revolutionary movement of the Akali Sikhs, became, according to Sir Michael O'Dwyer, the 'prominent members of the Babbar (lion) Akali gang responsible for a murderous campaign on Ghadr lines, in Jullundar, Ludhiana and Hoshiarpur'.[10] On the heroism and glorious sacrifices of the Babbar Akalis, Bhagat Singh published an article in *Pratap* on 15 March 1926.[11]

In his study, *Arya Dharma*, Kenneth Jones has shown that the Sikhs in Punjab were drawn to the Arya Samaj at the end of the nineteenth and early twentieth century because they found that the Arya Samaj like their own religious faith followed the tenets of monotheism, social equality, and justice.[12] Bhagat Singh's joining the National College (*Kaumi Vidya-pith*) marked a critical turning point in his intellectual political life. The National College was founded at Lahore by Lala Lajpat Rai during the Non-Cooperation movement, and Bhai Parmanand was appointed its Vice Chancellor. The college was not affiliated to the Punjab University nor did it have a regular teaching staff. Bhagat Singh's close association with his teachers Bhai Parmanand, Jaichandra Vidyalankar and Chhabil Das (later Principal) acted as an intellectual and moral stimulus on his life and inspired him to carve out his mission of life. According to Jaichandra Vidyalankar, Parmanand's lectures on European history fired the imagination of students in the college.[13] He was regarded as the living spirit of the college—'*vey to is ke praan they*' (his life-breath). He was not only a sound scholar of Indian and European history but an embodiment of patriotism, heroism, and sacrifice. Virendra Sindhu in her *Yugdrashta Bhagat Singh aur uske Mritunjay Purkha* states that Parmanand was particularly fond of Bhagat Singh. It was Parmanand who had arranged for Bhagat Singh's admission to the National College following a special examination in lieu of the matriculation examination.[14] During his college days Bhagat Singh was more drawn to the Irish revolutionary movement than the Russian Revolution.

Bhai Parmanand was an extraordinary man. He was a patriot, a freedom fighter, and a revolutionary. He was highly educated and learned. He interacted with some of the leading intellectuals and public men of his times. A Mohyal Brahmin hailing from Karyala in the district of Jhelum, Parmanand received his MA degree from Punjab University in 1902. A life-member of the D.A.V. College, Lahore, he joined the staff of the college as a lecturer in history and political economy. He was an inspiring teacher. The D.A.V. College management sent him abroad to collect funds for the development of the college, and to propagate the ideals of the Arya Samaj. Besides the duties entrusted to him, which he carried out with devotion, Parmanand continued his academic pursuits. Earlier he had joined Cambridge University, but later he went over to King's College, London, where he studied MA in History. However, he could not pass his examination because his thesis was not accepted.

Parmanand delivered his lectures on Vedic religion in South Africa and established three or four branches of the Arya Samaj there. Emily C. Brown, the biographer of Har Dyal, writes that during his visit to London, Parmanand had met V.D. Savarkar, who is reported to have brought him into the revolutionary movement.[15] Parmanand was one of the closest associates of Har Dyal. He stayed with Har Dyal for about a month at La Martineque (West Indies) when Har Dyal was thinking of founding a new religion, but Parmanand persuaded him to take to politics and shift his base of political activity to America.[16] Parmanand also studied for sometime in California University.

Kartar Singh Sarabha, a founding member of the Ghadr Party, recalled that it was Bhai Parmanand who had pushed him into the revolutionary movement and 'blessed his mission' when he had stayed with him in America.[17] Before the Ghadrites launched their campaign in Punjab, Sarabha accompanied Parmanand to Bengal to collect weapons to fight the British.[18] From the above examples cited on the revolutionary activities of Har Dyal and Kartar Singh Sarabha it is evident that Parmanand was capable of moulding the thought process of people. His *Twarikh-I-Hind* written in 1914 was proscribed by the British government in 1915. Implicated in the Lahore

Conspiracy Case, Parmanand was given the death sentence in 1915, which was later commuted to life imprisonment by the Viceroy Lord Hardinge. Due to the intercession of C.F. Andrews, he was released in 1920. On his return he joined the Non-Cooperation movement, and started teaching in the National College, where he came in close contact with Bhagat Singh. From the range, themes and type of books that Bhagat Singh studied, it is evident, especially from his prison notes, that Parmanand was the guiding spirit of Bhagat Singh's studies which was to open a new chapter in his political life.

Bhagat Singh was about twelve when the blood-curdling Jallianwala Bagh massacre took place. As a sensitive youth he was a witness to the stormy political events where his countrymen were handcuffed, tortured, arrested, and massacred during the brutal regime of Sir Michael O'Dwyer, the Lieutenant Governor of Punjab. Even some of the prominent businessmen, lawyers, and students were humiliated and tortured during this time.

Due to the scanty source-material, it is difficult to draw the intellectual profile of Bhagat Singh. Jitendra Nath Sanyal, a co-accused in the Lahore Conspiracy Case, and who knew him well wrote:

> Bhagat Singh was an extremely well-read man and his special sphere of study was Socialism. The batch of youngmen that figured in the Lahore Conspiracy Case was essentially an intellectual one. But even in this group Bhagat Singh predominated for his intellectual ascendancy. Though Socialism was his special subject, he had deeply studied the

history of the Russian revolutionary movement from its beginning in the early 19th century to the October Revolution of 1917. It is generally believed that very few in India could be compared to him in the knowledge of this special subject. The economic experiment in Russia under the Bolshevik regime also greatly interested him.[19]

Bhagat Singh had an enquiring mind. His curiosity was insatiable and he was always eager to learn. He wanted to know the how and why of things. His mind was active, yet not accumulative. A voracious reader, he read such books which he thought would resolve the multiple problems facing his country. The nature of readings listed in his prison notes show the bent of his mind. His quotations are drawn from the writings of Socrates, Plato, John Bodin, Thomas Acquines, Edmund Burke, John Locke, Thomas Paine, J.S. Mill, Spinoza, Jean-Jacques Rousseau, Marx, Fredrich Engels, Karl Kautsky, Fyodor Dostoevsky, Nikolai Bukharin, Lenin, Leon Trotsky, Omar Khayyam, and Bertrand Russell.[20]

Bhagat Singh's selection of books show that his main interest lay in understanding the rise and growth of human civilisation, socialism, the progressive development of revolutionary movements, the character of states, religion, the family, human rights, and internationalism. On patriotism, he quotes from Byron's 'Prisoner of Chillon', and Tennyson's 'A Charge of the Light Brigade'. From Tennyson's *Morte d'Arthur* he cities, 'The old order changeth yielding place to new.' He read Dostoevsky's *Crime and Punishment* and Victor Hugo's, *Les Misérables*. He reproduces verses from the poems of Arthur

Clough, who had unabated support of the revolutionaries.

The socialist Upton Sinclair's polemics *Oil* and *Boston* were his favourites.

Bhagat Singh also cites a number of quotations from Valentine Chirol's *India, Old and New* including an extract from Mahatma Gandhi's speech which he had delivered at the Nagpur session of the Indian National Congress in December 1920, which reads, 'The British will have to beware that if they do not want to do justice it will be the bounden duty of every Indian to destroy the Empire.'[21]

Bhagat Singh was candid enough to recognise in the following note the contribution of the Arya Samaj to the cause of national independence.

> However, the Arya Samaj in 1907 thought it wise to publish a resolution to the effect that as mischievous people here and there spread rumours hostile to them, the organization in reiterating its old creed, declared that it had no connection of any kind with any political body or with any political agitation in any shape. While accepting this declaration as disassociating the Samaj as a body from the extremist politics, it should be noted in fairness to the orthodox Hindus that while the Samaj does not include people more than 5% of the Hindu population of the Punjab, an enormous proportion, Hindus convicted of sedition and other political offences from 1907 down to the present day, are members of the Samaj.[22]

By the 1920s Bhagat Singh grew into a spirited and dashing young man of a mercurial temper and buoyant confidence, somewhat self-righteous and stubborn, overwhelmingly ambitious, and bumptious. He was open-minded and an incurable romantic, known for his boisterous laugh, and the use of some coarse Punjabi expletives with gusto in the company of his peers. He was earnest enough to scale new heights but equally carefree to indulge in trivialities. Bhagat Singh was one of such young men who are born to give no rest to themselves, and to give none to others.

Bhagat Singh saw some hope for political advancement in Gandhi's Non-Cooperation movement, which he had launched to shatter the prestige of the British government and to paralyse it. But Gandhi's withdrawal of the movement due to the Chauri Chaura incident on 5 February 1922 disillusioned him with the Gandhian brand of politics. It was not only Bhagat Singh but many religiously-minded and radical nationalists like Jawaharlal Nehru and Subhas Chandra Bose who felt unhappy and angry at Gandhi's withdrawal of Non-Cooperation. Bhagat Singh thought that Gandhi's mode of fighting the British through non-violence was primitive and behind the times. He held that age must be respected, and experience valued, but when age falls into passivity and languor and warps judgements, then a new course of action should be called for. The years 1922-24 were further marred by the rise of communal riots in the country, which vitiated Hindu-Muslim relations.[23]

There were eleven riots in 1923, eighteen in 1924, sixteen in 1925, thirty-five in 1926, and thirty-one upto November 1927. In 1926, the first year of Lord Irwin's term as Viceroy, forty riots took place. After the Kohat riot in 1924, Gandhi undertook a twenty-one-day fast. The communal problem had become a bugbear of Indian leadership, and seemed to defy any solution during the 1920s. The Nehru Report (1928), Jinnah's Fourteen Points (March 1928), and the All Parties Conference (December 1929) and the Simon Commission proposals (May 1930) could not settle the communal problem, which, in Gandhi's words, became a 'problem of problems'. The basic question was of Muslim representation as a minority community in the new constitutional arrangements that were to be made at the provincial and central level.

Bhagat Singh witnessed the collapse of the Gandhian movement of Non-Cooperation. He also saw the spirit of communal violence vitiating the atmosphere in the country. He mocked the constitutional way of promoting the cause of self-rule as advocated by moderates like Sir Tej Bahadur Sapru and M.R. Jayakar. He condemned the futility of constitutional wrangling among the political parties. Driven by the thought that the Indian political leaders were frittering away their energies, he looked to Marxism as the panacea for all the ills from which India suffered. Bhagat Singh and his associates were conscious of the terrible backwardness and low political development of the population, which was living under conditions of exploitation and oppression.

Bhagat Singh joined the Hindustan Socialist Republican Association (HRSA) and was elected the general secretary of its central committee. The plunge into active politics brought him substantially in touch with left-wing literature, especially the writings of Lenin and Marx. He took to journalism and wrote several articles in the vernacular press, in Urdu and Punjabi. He also worked with Pratap Press and the Hindi daily *Vir Arjun*. In March 1926, Bhagat Singh founded the Naujawan

Bharat Sabha of Lahore to infuse revolutionary ideas among the youth. Comrade Ram Chander was appointed the president of the Sabha with Bhagat Singh as its secretary, and Bhagwati Charan Vohra its treasurer. The objective of the Naujawan Bharat Sabha was to establish an independent socialist republic of peasants and workers by all possible means, and to mobilise peasants and workers for fervent political activities. Bhagat Singh projected a clear vision of waging an armed rebellion against the British power. The Manifesto of the Hindustan Republican Association and the constitution of the Hindustan Republican Association make it clear that Bhagat Singh and his comrades had a clear-cut plan for collecting armed weapons and ammunition, and making them readily available, when necessary. Their ultimate aim was to establish a Federal Republic of the United States of India by seizing power through a well-organised armed revolution. Bhagat Singh was arrested in connection with the Dussehra bomb outrage in 1926, and locked up in a small cell on 17 December 1928.

Bhagat Singh and Rajguru shot dead a twenty-two-year-old British officer, John Poyantz Saunders, the assistant superintendent. Saunder's *munshi*, Chanan Singh too was shot and he died just opposite the principal's office, D.A.V.College. While dying he said, '*Sahib, main mara gaya*' (Sahib, I am dying). Possibly he was shot by Chandra Shekhar Azad. The next day Bhagat Singh and his comrades put up posters in different parts of the town reiterating the tyranny of the British government and the determination of the Indian people to continue their struggle for power.[24] Saunders was just getting on his red motorcycle, when he was shot dead at 4 pm. He had been in India for about a year. This incident occurred a month and half after Lala Lajpat Rai was assaulted by *lathi* blows when he was leading a procession in protest against the Simon Commission near the Lahore railway station. On 17 November 1928 as a result of the injuries received, Lala Lajpat Rai died. Saunders was one of the officers who had helped to restrain the crowd from the barrier of the Lahore railway station, on 30 October 1928 at 12.30 pm.

On 8 April 1929 at 12.30 pm, Bhagat Singh and Batukeshwar Dutt threw two bombs in the Central Assembly chamber along with leaflets outlining their aims, and exposing the hypocrisy of the British devices to hoodwink the Indian people with false promises.[25] Ironically, Sir John Simon, whose Commission had inflamed the country, was also present at the Assembly. Bhagat Singh and Batukeshwar Dutt offered themselves for arrest shouting *'Inquilab Zindabad!'* (Long Live the Revolution). Later, Bhagat Singh, Raj Guru and Sukhdev were hanged in Lahore Central Jail on 23 March 1931 at 7.30 pm, six days before the Congress Session at Karachi.

Notes

1. Jitendra Nath Sanyal, in *Bhagat Singh: A Biography*, K.C. Yadav, Babar Singh (ed.) pp. 23-24.
2. *Selected Works of Motilal Nehru*, vol. 7 (1929-31), Ravinder Kumar and Hari Dev Sharma (eds.), pp. 150-51.
3. Ibid.
4. Jawaharlal Nehru, *An Autobiography*, p. 192.
5. Bhai Parmanand, *Ap, Biti* (Urdu) p. 53.

6. Bhagat Singh, in *The Fragrance of Freedom*, K.C. Yadav and Babar Singh (eds.), p. 198, also in *Kirti*, March 1928.
7. 'The Martyrs of the Delhi Conspiracy Case', in *The Fragrance of Freedom*, K.C. Yadav and Babar Singh (eds.), p. 190-95.
8. Sir Michael O'Dwyer, *India as I knew It*, (1885-1925, 1925), pp. 190-209.
9. Bhagat Singh, 'Kartar Singh Sarabha', in *The Fragrance of Freedom*, in K.C. Yadav and Babar Singh, (eds.), pp. 143-50, *Chand*, November 1928.
10. Sir Michael O'Dwyer, *India as I knew It*, p. 209.
11. 'The Sacrifices of the Babbar Akalis' in *The Fragrance of Freedom*, K.C. Yadav and Babar Singh (eds.), pp. 121-27.
12. Kenneth Jones, *Arya Dharma: Hindu Consciousness* in 19th Century Punjab, 1988, pp. 136-39.
13. Recollections of Comrade Ram Chander in *Bhagat Singh: Making of a Revolutionary: Contemporary Portrayals*, K.C. Yadav and Babar Singh (eds.), p. 200.
14. Virendra Sindhu, *Yugdrashtra Bhagat Singh and Uske Mritunjany Purkha*, p. 146.
15. Emily C. Brown, *Har Dyal Hindu Revolutionary and Rationalist*, p. 24.
16. Harish Puri, *Ghadar Movement, Ideology, Organisation and Stragegy*, p. 55, see Chaman Lal, *Ghadar Party Nayak, Kartar Singh Saraba* (Hindi), pp. 3, 6-9, 10, 35, 99-101, 120-21.
17. *Arya Samaj and the Freedom Movement*, vol. I, *1875-1918*, K.C.Yadav and K.S. Arya, (eds.), pp. 220-21, of Bhai Parmanand's close affiliations with Kartar Singh Sarabha in Ghadar movement, see Chaman Lal, *Ghadar Party Nayak, Kartar Singh Sarabha* (Hindi) pp. 3, 6-9, 10, 35, 99-101, 120-21.
18. Puri, p. 163.
19. Jintendra Nath Sanyal, *Bhagat Singh: A Biography*, K.C. Yadav and Babar Singh (eds.), p. 105.

20. For an incisive analysis of Bhagat Singh's notebook, see L.V. Mitrokin 'The Last Days of Bhagat Singh' in *Lenin in India*, L.V. Mitrokin (ed.), pp. 115-34.
21. *Bhagat Singh papers*, p. 140. (Nehru Memorial Museum and Library).
22. Ibid., p. 141, Bhagat Singh: The Ideas on Freedom, Liberty and Resolution: *Jails Notes of a Revolutionary*, K.C. Yadav and Babar Singh (eds.), p. 295
23. V.N. Datta, 'Bhagat Singh', in the *Tribune*, 18 March 2007.
24. Appendix I.
25. Appendix II.

3

Gandhi's Attitude

There was no question of Gandhi's approving or commending Bhagat Singh's killing J.P. Saunders, or his throwing bombs at the Central Assembly hall. His soul revolted against such brutal deeds. Because of his firm adherence to the doctrine of non-violence, which he regarded as an article of his faith, and a passion of his existence, he could never make the commutation of Bhagat Singh's death sentence a precondition for signing his Pact with Viceroy Irwin. Subhas Chandra Bose wrote in his autobiography that he pleaded with the Mahatma to break with the Viceroy on the question of Bhagat Singh's death sentence. Subhas Chandra Bose recalls:

> I ventured the suggestion that he (Gandhi) should, if necessary, to break with the Viceroy on the question because the execution was against the spirit, if not the letter of the Delhi Pact. I was reminded of a similar incident during the

armistice between the Sinn Fein Party and the British government when the strong attitude adopted by the former secured the release of Irish political prisoners sentenced to the gallows. But the Mahatma, who did not wish to identify himself with the revolutionary prisoners, would not go so far, and it naturally made a great difference when the Viceroy realized that the Mahatma would not break on that question.[1]

Why couldn't the Mahatma break the Pact, Bose asks? Subhas Chandra Bose's poser needs an answer. Nearly three decades earlier in 1909, Gandhi had severely denounced Madan Lal Dhingra's killing of Sir William Curzon Wyllie, Aide-de-Camp to the Secretary of State, Lord Morley on 1 July 1909 in the Institute of Imperial Studies, London. Gandhi regarded Dhingra as a misguided youth, whose sacrifice was futile and who gave his body (he was subsequently hanged) in a wrong way and its ultimate result was mischievous.[2] Condemning the use of violence in political strategy, Gandhi wrote, 'One of the accepted and time-bound methods to attain the end is that of violence. The assassination of Sri Curzon Wyllie was an illustration in its worst and most detestable form of that method (of violence).'[3] Gandhi firmly believed that Dhingra's action had done grievous harm to his country by his ignoble act. He rejected completely the 'cult of violence' expounded and preached by V.D. Savarkar and his associates in London for the liberation of the country from foreign rule.

When Dhingra's case came to the old Bailey, Gandhi was in England. He sent his views on Wyllie's murder for publication in the *Indian Opinion* in Natal which appeared in its issue of 14 August 1909. Gandhi had gone to England in a delegation to lobby for the interests of the Transval Asians, who were suffering from social discrimination, and to campaign against the notorious 'Black Ordinance' requiring the registration of Asiatics.

During his stay in London from July 1909 to November 1909, Gandhi gave serious thought to understand the motives and nature of Dhingra's action. The Dhingra case and his hanging made a profound impact on Gandhi's thinking, and acted as a stimulus to the formation and evolution of his moral and political philosophy. Discussing the Dhingra case, and the circumstances under which he committed the murder in a state of intoxication, Gandhi drew the following conclusion:

> I must say that those who believe and argue that such murders may do good to India are ignorant men indeed. No act of treachery can ever profit a nation. Even should the British leave in consequence of such murderous acts, who will rule in their place? The only answer is: the murderers. Who will then be happy? Is the Englishman bad because he is an Englishman? Is it that everyone with an Indian skin is good? If that is so, we can claim no rights in South Africa, nor should there be any angry protest against oppression by Indian princes. India can gain nothing from the rule of murderers—no matter whether they are black or white. Under such a rule, India will be utterly ruined and laid waste. This train of thought leads to a host of reflections, but I have no time to set them down here. I am afraid some Indians will commend this murder. I believe they will be guilty of a heinous sin. We ought to abandon such fanciful ideas.[4]

In his letter dated 14 October 1909 to H.S.L. Polak who was in London, Gandhi wrote:

> It will be your duty to tell the revolutionaries and everybody else that the freedom they want or they think that they want, is not to be obtained by killing people or doing violence but by setting themselves right and by becoming and remaining truly Indian.[5]

Making his way back to Natal, on the ship *Kildonan Castle*, Gandhi wrote in ten days, 13 to 22 November 1909, his pamphlet *Hind Swaraj*, which laid the foundation of his political thought. Originally written in Gujarati, it was published in the columns of the *Indian Opinion* in South Africa on 11 and 18 December 1909. It was issued as a booklet in January 1910 and its English version appeared in 1910. It was proscribed by the Government of India on 24 March 1910. The *Hind Swaraj* projected a moral and political system. It propagated universal values such as Absolute Truth, non-violence (*Ahimsa*) and *Dharma*. This work provides a gist of Gandhi's political and economic thought. The *Hind Swaraj* can be called Gandhi's *Meditations* like Jesus Christ's *Sermon on the Mount* or Rousseau's *Social Contract*. Gandhi regarded the *Hind Swaraj* as the right and proper answer to the anarchists in London, who were advocating the cult of violence for the liberation of the country from foreign rule. The cardinal principle that the *Hind Swaraj* advocated was that the use of violent means for the attainment of political ideals, however laudable, was suicidal, and that a strict adherence to the doctrine of non-violence was the only way to solve India's manifold complicated problems, including, how to free the country from foreign bondage.

All his life Gandhi stuck to the path of non-violence with an iron-will. He regarded non-violence a religion, a way of life, and the central organising principle of Hinduism, which embodies the highest human values such as compassion, charity, and forgiveness.[6] According to his interpretation, the message of the *Gita* is non-violence. He had emphasised in the *Hind Swaraj* that the adoption of non-violence as a political strategy and theory of self-purification would elevate the national movement at a higher moral level, bringing forth immense benefits to the struggle for India's freedom. In fact, he firmly believed that non-violence was the most suitable and efficacious weapon for breaking the British power in India. Gandhi comes out of his *Hind Swaraj* as a strict moral scientist, who abhorred violence because he was firmly convinced that it would never achieve lasting results. He wanted to write the *History of India* from a non-violent perspective, showing the power and benefits that would accrue by following non-violent means through successive stages in India's fight for freedom.

Gandhi would have no truck with Madan Lal Dhingra's way of fighting the British through violent means because he thought that such methods were suicidal, quasi-Machiavellian, devoid of morality, and immensely harmful to India's cause of freedom. He believed that Dhingra's use of violence for political purposes, which may be called terrorism or militancy, was individualistic, involved no masses, and left no scope for negotiations, parley or settlement with British authorities. Exposing the ill-fated consequences of violent means, Gandhi argued that a terrorist or a militant nationalist kills surreptiously (which is in itself an immoral act) is caught, and then hanged, losing his life thoughtlessly, with no gain to himself or to the country he dies for.

When Lord Hardinge, the Viceroy, was making his ceremonial entry into the new capital (Delhi) on 23 December 1912, a bomb was thrown at him which injured him. Gandhi felt distressed about the incident, and wrote a strongly-worded short note entitled 'A Catastrophe' in the *Indian Opinion* dated 28 December 1912, which is as follows:

A Catastrophe

We have to thank our stars that the dastardly act of the bomb-thrower at Delhi did not prove fatal to Lord Hardinge's life and that Lady Hardinge had a miraculous escape. That in this century, which is considered an enlightened period in the history of mankind, there are people who believe that assassination can lead to political or other reform is a fact which should make people think and ask whether what passes under the name of progress is real progress. We as Indians deplore that this nefarious institution of cold-blooded Satanic murder should find its votaries in India. We cannot recall instances of the kind in Indian history. Assassination for selfish ends is as old as the hills. It had its sway in India also long before the introduction, in that land, of Western influence. But political assassination is a recent excrescence in the life of India. The mad youth who perpetrated the crime no doubt thought that by striking murders of distinguished men, rulers could be terrorized and an independent India could be thereby secured. We should decline to share any such independence even if it were attainable, which we doubt. We do not believe that good can be brought about by evil.

The fact is that the idea of securing independence by assassination is chimerical. The result can only be greater repression, greater suspicion on the part of the rulers, greater taxation on the people, and consequent increase in the hardships of the poorest in the land. In the midst of this darkness we can but pray for India's deliverance from the curse of assassination and the return of the few misguided youths to the sane teaching of their forefathers that freedom comes only from self-suffering and purification—never by inflicting suffering on others. We pray, too, for Lord Hardinge's quick recovery from the effect of the wound received by him.[7]

In the mid-1920s, Gandhi used to keep a record of his multifarious activities meticulously. From his notes it is evident that he was a voracious reader of books, and his favourite authors were Tolstoy, Ruskin, and Thoreau. He also read a good deal of ancient Hindu scriptures, which stirred his thoughts. By virtue of his creative ability in assimilating and synthesising ideas drawn from various literary sources, he produced a unique individualistic paradigm based on non-violence to meet the social, political crises that confronted him. Immersed in following the instructions of Patanjali's *Yoga Sutra* which laid down the principle of reaching the summit of self-perfectibility through non-violence, non-possession of material objects, purification of self, and control of sexual passions, Gandhi believed that he would be capable of winning battles and conquering his adversaries.

At the Lahore Congress session held on 31 December 1929, while congratulating Lord Irwin and Lady Irwin on their safety when a bomb was thrown on their white Vicergal train outside the Delhi railway station on 23 December 1929, Gandhi moved the following resolution which condemned the terrorist activities:

> The Congress deplores the bomb outrage perpetrated on the Viceroy's train and reiterates its conviction that such action is not only contrary to the creed of the Congress but results in harm being done to the national cause. It congratulates the Viceroy and Lady Irwin and their party including the poor servants on their fortunate and narrow escape.[8]

The Resolution was passed despite strong opposition for which Gandhi made a strong plea. He said:

> We lose nothing by using common courtesy, Not only so; we would be guilty of not having understood the implications of our creed if we forget that these Englishmen, whether in authority or who choose to remain in India, are our charge, that we who profess this creed of non-violence, should consider ourselves trustees for the safety of their lives.[9]

The Resolution was carried.

Due to the initiative of the Labour government headed by Prime Minister Ramsay MacDonald (1937-1986?), which took a sympathetic view of the aspirations of the Indian people for self-government, and the mediation of prominent Indian liberals such as Sir Tej Bahadur Sapru, Mr Jayakar and Srinivasa Sastri, Gandhi was released from prison on 26 January 1931. He had been arrested for launching the Civil Disobedience movement in 1930. Various explanations have been given by historians for Gandhi's calling off the Civil Disobedience movement. Sumit Sarkar maintains that the crucial reason for Gandhi's withdrawing the Civil Disobedience movement was the strong commercial pressure put on him by business magnates like G.D. Birla, Walchand Hirachand, and Purshottamdas Thakurdas who thought that the further continuance of the anti-British struggle would adversely affect their commercial interests.[10] Two considerations probably weighed on Gandhi in calling off the Civil Disobedience movement. Firstly, he realised that the campaign was petering out for lack of support; and secondly, he thought that it would be imprudent to miss the opportunity to participate in the forthcoming Round Table Conference in London (the first he had missed) when the crucial question of Indian's constitutional advancement to self-rule was going to be considered.

The Gandhi-Irwin talks began on a man-to-man basis on 18 February 1931, and ended on 5 March 1931. They focused on some of the crucial issues facing the country. Gandhi met the Viceroy eight times and spent nearly twenty-two hours in negotiating a settlement with him. In the early hours of 5 March, the Gandhi-Irwin Pact was signed.[11] Jawaharlal Nehru, the Congress President, was disappointed with the Pact. On learning about the details of the Pact, he felt 'great emptiness', in his heart.[12] He wrote:

On the night of the 4th March, we waited till midnight for Gandhiji's return from the Viceroy's house. He came about 2 am and we were woken up and told that an agreement had been reached.[13]

Robert Bernays, a senior journalist working for the *News Chronicle*, London, maintained a diary during his five-month stay in India during 1931, which provides a blow-by-blow account of the negotiations conducted between Gandhi and Lord Irwin.[14] His diary entitled *Naked Faquir*, the expression Winston Churchill had used for Gandhi, was published in 1931 and ran into three editions in the very first year of its publication. He met a number of prominent Indian political leaders and top-ranking British civil and military officials, and recorded his discussions with them on the current political issues. His diary, brilliantly written, so packed with detail, compels respect, and most of it rings true. Bernays comes out of his diary as a sensitive and accurate political analyst and a sharp judge of men and affairs.

The Pact stipulated that (1) the Congress would call off the Civil Disobedience movement and participate in the next Round Table Conference to draw up a future Federal Constitution for 'Self-governing' India with safeguards; (2) release all the prisoners not charged with violence during the Civil Disobedience movement; (3) immediate stoppage of repression; (4) restitution of confiscated property and the reinstatement of government servants; and (5) salt manufacture to be permitted on the coast and to remit taxes not already paid. The issue of independence or dominion status for India was not incorporated in the Pact. Nor was the issue of Bhagat Singh's death sentence mentioned in the Pact.[15]

What passed between Gandhi and Irwin during their twenty-two-hour negotiation is not recorded. But it is clear from their correspondence and public statements that Gandhi was deeply concerned about the question of Bhagat Singh's death sentence. It was not an easy task for Gandhi to broach the Bhagat Singh subject, which involved the murder of a British police officer. A votary of non-violence, he was to take up the subject of major political issues relating to the country; and dealing with such a highly sensitive issue of the commutation of Bhagat Singh's death sentence required caution, subtlety, patience, and tact.

Gandhi took up the question of Bhagat Singh's death sentence on 18 February 1931. He moved the matter subtly and cautiously in camera, discussing the issue with the Viceroy, and putting pressure on him step by step. Irwin's note makes it clear that Gandhi was opposed to capital punishment in principle, but the Viceroy writes that at their first meeting Gandhi did not ask for the commutation of Bhagat Singh's death sentence.[16] Gandhi then pleaded that the commutation would have 'influence', and further, that on his own he would have commuted Bhagat Singh's death sentence.[17] In his interview to the Press, he criticised the 'evil of capital punishment', which disables a person to reform himself. He also assured the public that on the Bhagat Singh case, 'I put it (to the Viceroy) as a "humanitarian issue", and desired the suspension (of death sentence) so that there may not be turmoil in the country.'[18] He thought that every person, even if he has committed murder, must be given an opportunity to reform himself. He condemned the notion of retributive justice which is based on an-eye-for-an-eye which makes the world blind.

In his letter to the Viceroy dated 23 March, Gandhi made a last desperate effort to save Bhagat Singh's life, which was dispatched to him by a special messenger. Gandhi wrote:

> Popular opinion rightly or wrongly demands commutation. When there is no principle at stake, it is often a duty to respect it.
>
> In the present case the chances are that, if commutation is granted, internal peace is most likely to be promoted. In the event of execution, peace is undoubtedly in danger.
>
> Seeing that I am able to inform you that the revolutionary party has assured me that, in the event of these lives being spared, that party will stay its hands, suspension of sentence pending cessation of revolutionary murders becomes in my opinion a peremptory duty.
>
> Political murders have been condoned before now. It is worthwhile saving these lives, if thereby many other innocent lives are likely to be saved and may be even revolutionary crime almost stamped out.
>
> Since you seem to value my influence such as it is in favour of peace, do not please unnecessarily make my position, difficult as it is, almost too difficult for future work.
>
> Execution is an irretrievable act. If you think there is the slightest chance of error of judgement, I would urge you to suspend for further review an act that is beyond recall.
>
> If my presence is necessary, I can come. Though I may not speak I may hear and write what I want to say 'Charity never faileth'.[19]

The last line of the letter written in true Christian spirit was intended to arouse compassionate feelings in the mind of Irwin, who himself was a staunch Anglican. In this letter Gandhi urged the Viceroy to 'suspend for further review an act that is beyond recall'. This request does not mean that Gandhi wanted only suspension and not the commutation of the death sentence. His intention was to stall the commutation of the death sentence for the time being so that he could gain time to get the whole question of Bhagat Singh's death sentence reviewed. From the above letter it is evident that Gandhi still hoped that the death sentence would be commuted to life imprisonment. Gandhi suggested to the Viceroy that he was still willing to meet him, implying that Bhagat Singh's case mattered a great deal to him. In fact, Gandhi was willing to postpone his departure from Delhi.

Irwin too endorses that Gandhi made concerted efforts to save Bhagat Singh's life. In his farewell speech delivered at Chelmsford Club, New Delhi on 27 March 1931, Irwin said:

> As I listened the other day to Mr Gandhi putting the case for commutation forcefully before me, I reflected first, of what significance it surely was that the apostle of non-violence so earnestly be pleading the cause of a creed so opposite to his own. But I should regard it as wholly wrong in allowing the matter to be influenced or deflected by purely political considerations.[20]

While reflecting on his negotiations with Gandhi later, Irwin wrote in his memoir:

> He (Gandhi) was just going off to the meeting of the Congress at Karachi which he hoped would satisfy our agreement, and he wished to appeal for the life of a young man called Bhagat Singh who had recently been condemned to death for various terrorist crimes. He was himself opposed to capital punishment but that was not now in debate. If the young man was hanged, said Mr Gandhi, there was likelihood that he would become a national martyr and the general atmosphere would be prejudiced. I told him that, while I quite appreciated his feelings in the matter, I also was not concerned with the merits or demerits of capital punishment, since my only duty was to work the law as I understood it. On that basis I could not conceive anyone who had more thoroughly deserved capital punishment than Bhagat Singh.[21]

Irwin further goes on to say that Gandhi 'greatly feared unless I could do something about it (death sentence), the effect would be to destroy our Pact, I said I should regret that no less than he'.[22] Finally, Irwin tells Gandhi that 'it was impossible for me from my point of view to grant him (Bhagat Singh) reprieve'.[23]

Of the Indian political leaders none spoke in public with such passion and eloquence of Bhagat Singh's patriotism, courage and fearlessness as Jawaharlal Nehru. Bhagat Singh's death sentence posed a serious problem for Nehru. What position should he take? There lay a conflict in his mind. He admired Bhagat Singh and his associates who were bold enough to die for the love of their country. Bhagat Singh too like Nehru was committed to the creed of Socialism. Nehru's charismatic personality as a leader of the youth fascinated Bhagat Singh. Nehru marvelled at the high spirits which Bhagat Singh and his comrades showed, when he met them in the Central Jail in Lahore. They were then on a hunger strike, which he thought, had 'aroused new political consciousness in the country'.[24] In his public speeches he claimed that the Congress did its best to save Bhagat Singh's life. He said, 'We made every effort for the release of Bhagat Singh.'[25]

Mohammed Ali Jinnah, a secular-minded and firm Indian nationalist, took up the cause of the political prisoners involved in the Lahore Conspiracy Case. Condemning the Public Safety Bill and the Trade Disputes Bill on 12 and 14 September 1929 as unjust and totally unwarranted, he made a strong appeal to the government to treat decently the accused Bhagat Singh and his associates, who were not convicts then.[26] In support of his contention, he quoted the principle of justice observed by decent civilised society, '...man is taken to be innocent until he is proved to be guilty, and no one is to be condemned until he is given a hearsay'.[27] Denouncing the Punjab government as having no brain and acting in a brutal manner, Jinnah asked the government to satisfy the demands of the prisoners, who were demanding only the 'bare necessities of life'. He was sympathetic to the prisoners who, he thought, were the 'creatures of circumstances'. But Jinnah totally disapproved the use of violent means in any form of political activity. As a strict constitutionalist, he remained completely silent, when the death sentence of Bhagat Singh was announced.

In 1919, Rabindranath Tagore, had renounced his Knighthood to the government in protest against the Jallianwala

Bagh massacre committed by General Dyer's action at Amritsar on 13 April 1919, and the Martial Law atrocities inflicted on the people under the Lieutenant Governor Sir Michael O'Dwyer's regime. On Bhagat Singh's trial and death sentence, like Jinnah, Tagore too remained completely silent.

Asaf Ali, a prominent member of the Congress party, acted as Bhagat Singh's lawyer in the Central Legislative Assembly bomb case. In fact, he was present in the Assembly when the bombs were thrown. Recollecting the past events leading to the Gandhi-Irwin Pact, Asaf Ali writes that much pressure was put on Gandhi to secure reprieve for Bhagat Singh and his comrades after they had been sentenced to death, but 'the Mahatma did not find it consistent with his creed of non-violence to mak it a part of his Pact'.[28] But Asaf Ali acknowledges that Gand' did whatever he could to persuade the Viceroy to commute the death sentence. Asaf Ali gives some details about the efforts that the Mahatma made. He wrote:

> A day before we left for Karachi I approached Mahatmaji and showed him the draft which I had made to be signed by Bhagat Singh and others circumstantially signifying a repudiation of the cult of violence should they agree to do so, that after that it might be easier for Gandhiji to plead reprieve. I felt that Bhagat Singh had considerable regard for me and I argued with him that he might renounce violence.[29]

Assured by Bhagat Singh and others that they would renounce violence, Asaf Ali went to Gandhi who advised him to approach the authorities. Gandhi amended Asaf Ali's draft. Asaf Ali further writes:

I went to Lahore and phoned up the Home Secretary and told him the purpose of my mission and requested him to let me have an interview with Bhagat Singh. The Home Secretary was extremely polite and expressed his regret that the Government would not allow me to interview Bhagat Singh. That was the last effort that I made on behalf of Bhagat Singh.[30]

Aruna Asaf Ali maintains that Gandhi had 'interceded, through letters, and in person for securing commutation of the death sentence that was passed on Bhagat Singh and his comrades'.[31] A retraction of belief, in violent means, she adds, could have secured commutation, but Bhagat Singh was not the person made of that stuff. She emphasises that 'Gandhij was unstinting in praise of the heroism but also uncompromising in reaffirming his disapproval of the path of violence.'[32] Mira Behn, Gandhi's confidant, reminiscing Bhagat Singh's execution wrote:

Bapu (Gandhi) did his best to obtain a reprieve, and though the Viceroy could give no definite assurance, still Bapu hoped and believed the remission would be granted, especially as the execution at such a moment would greatly intensify the anti-British feeling of the public.[33]

Sarojani Naidu told the *News Chronicle* journalist Robert Bernays, 'I admit that he (Bhagat Singh) ought to be punished for his crimes, but not by death. After all he is only a rebel.'[34]

From the above extracts on the Gandhi-Irwin correspondence and other contemporary evidence, it is clear that Gandhi was deeply interested in saving Bhagat Singh's life, and was consistent in his appeals to Irwin not to hang him. He disapproved Bhagat Singh's action, and thought it ruinous for the freedom of the country. He drew a clear distinction between Bhagat Singh's intentions and his actions. In the case of Madan Lal Dhingra's killing Sir Curzon Wyllie, Gandhi had made a scathing denunciation of his action but that was not Gandhi's attitude to Bhagat Singh's shooting. In 1909 when Dhingra shot Wyllie, Gandhi had not then conceived and evolved his doctrine of non-violence. With the intensity and maturity of his political experiences, he developed a benign and humanistic outlook which explains why he appealed to Irwin for the commutation of Bhagat Singh's death sentence purely on humanitarian grounds, while repudiating the use of violent means in any form of political activity.

Gandhi appealed to the Viceroy on moral grounds also because he thought that capital punishment is evil, and rules out the possibility for the guilty to reform himself. Further, Gandhi urged Irwin to commute the death sentence on pragmatic grounds; as such a worthy concession on the part of the government in reducing the punishment would ease the surcharged political atmosphere and create a congenial climate for conciliation between the government and Indian political parties. Robert Bernays who was close to Gandhi during his negotiations with the Viceroy wrote, 'Gandhi knew that there was no ground for reprieve in the case of Bhagat Singh but he appealed to him on humane grounds.'[35] However, he never made the staying of the executions a part of his agremeement with Irwin.

Critics such as Subhas Bose have argued that if Gandhi had made the commutation of Bhagat Singh's death sentence a precondition for signing the Gandhi-Irwin Pact, then Bhagat Singh's life could have been saved. But how could Gandhi do so after his commitment to non-violence? Fundamental to his whole life was the doctrine of non-violence! Freedom of the country could wait for him, but he would never give up, even for a moment his faith in non-violence. Furthermore, the Congress too claimed to adhere to the policy of non-violence in its struggle for freedom. This explains why he did not launch a Satyagraha movement or undertake a fast for the commutation of the death sentence because resorting to such actions would have allied him to use violent means in political activity.

Writers such as Manmathnath Gupta, as pointed out earlier, emphasise that Gandhi was not all emotionally involved in the imminent hanging of the three youths. To corroborate this view, they cite Gandhi's letter to the Home Secretary, H.W. Emerson, dated 20 March 1931.[36] Emerson wrote:

> Thank you for your letter just received. I know of the meeting you refer to. I have taken every precaution possible and hope that nothing untoward will happen. I suggest that there should be no display of police force and no interference in the meeting. Irritation is likely to be there. It will be better to allow it find vent through meetings, etc.

Some writers such as D.P. Das and Manmathnath Gupta draw the inference from the letter that Gandhi was supporting the government for maintaining peace while Bhagat Singh was going to be executed. To these writers such an attitude was a betrayal to the cause of the rebels. There does not seem any inconsistency in Gandhi's view. He was trying both for the commutation of Bhagat Singh's death sentence while at the same time trying to maintain law and order in the politically tense atmosphere. When the question of Bhagat Singh's death sentence was hung in the balance, and his fate was going to be decided, Emerson, as the Home Secretary, thought it his responsibility to ensure that public meetings organised in sympathy for Bhagat Singh and his associates, should remain peaceful without manifesting any spirit of violence and disturbance, and for this purpose he sought Gandhi's support. Emerson's well-meaning necessary steps and Gandhi's advice should not be mixed up, and seen independently of what was passing between Irwin and Gandhi on the question of Bhagat Singh's death commutation.

Gandhi's letter dated 2 March 1930 addressed to the Viceroy shows that he was deeply concerned about the radical political activities, which were gaining strength in the country. Gandhi wrote:

> It is common cause that, however disorganized and, for the time being, insignificant it may be, the party of violence is gaining ground and making itself felt. Its end is the same as mine. But I am convinced that it cannot bring the desired relief to the dumb millions.[37]

Several revolutionary organisations sprang up in various parts of the country, particularly in Punjab, Bengal and the United Provinces during this time. The most influential of these political bodies was the Hindustan Republican Army with which Bhagat Singh was closely associated. S. Gopal points out that there was a growing influence of Communism among the youth.[38]

The Communist Party was founded in 1925 and affiliated to the International in 1925. Gopal writes that 'there was hardly a single public service or industry, which was not affected by Communism, and factory workers of all types, coal miners, policemen, and even scavengers were all subjected to, and frequently succumbed to the influence of Communist feelings'.[39]

Faiz Ahmad Faiz, the renowned Urdu poet, who was then about twenty, recalls the impact of Communism on the youth of his own generation. He wrote:

> In the 1920s, if not on the streets, then certainly among young people, there was talk of Lenin, socialism and revolution. In the subcontinent, those were the days of the terrorist movement. In every household people talked about the Chittagong Army Case, the Kakori Dacoity Case, and of Bhagat Singh, Azad and Sher Jang. The Meerut Conspiracy Case we were already familiar with. In the Bhagat Singh movement, a couple of my friends were involved, led by Khawaja Khurshid Anwar, later to become a famous music director. My room in the hostel was his dumping ground for revolutionary literature. Most of these writings related to Karl Marx, Lenin and the Russian Revolution. Off and on, I would take a cursory look at them. Almost every day someone would stick a revolutionary poster on the college notice board; and sometimes these posters would come tucked into the pages of the daily newspaper. Under the influence of this revolutionary movement, public meetings had also undergone a change and instead of slogans of *Swaraj* and *Bande Matram*, one would hear shouts of *Inqilab*

Zindabad and instead of '*Saray Jahan se achha, Hindustan harmara*', one heard (Bhagat Singh's anthem) '*Sar katanay ki tammanna abb hamaray dil mein hai*'.[40]

Gandhi realised that within his own party some of its active members were firmly committed to the Socialist ideology, especially Nehru and Subhas Chandra Bose, who wanted a more radical approach to the solution of India's political problems. After his European visit in 1927, Nehru had turned into, what Gopal calls 'a self-conscious revolutionary radical'. It was due to the left-wing pressure at the Madras Congress 1927 that a resolution for complete independence for India was passed, which Gandhi criticised as 'hastily conceived and thoughtlessly passed'. In his letter to Nehru, Gandhi deplored, that he (Nehru) was 'moving too fast like an angry young man in a desperate hurry without taking into consideration the consequences of his actions'.[41] Gandhi thought that Nehru might, if unchecked, throw in his lot with the left-wing radicals, and to curb his revolutionary tendencies, he worked out a scheme for his election as the president of the Congress.

In October 1929, Nehru's Socialist friend, Virendranath Chattopadhyaya, wrote to him on his election to the Congress Presidency:

> When the cunning Mahatmaji proposed your name for the Presidency of the Congress, it was obvious that it was a move to kill you and the opposition.... In your new position of President-elect on the initiative of Gandhi, your hands will be completely tied, and any action that you might have otherwise taken as a leader of the independence movement

will be paralysed by the necessity of having to remain impartial inside the Congress.[42]

In Gandhi's calculation, there was no place for the radical left-wing politics, to which Bhagat Singh too was committed, yet he had appealed to the Viceroy for the commutation of Bhagat Singh's death sentence because of his opposition to capital punishment.

Notes

1. Subhas Chandra Bose, *The Indian Struggle*, p. 204.
2. V.N. Datta, *Madan Lal Dhingra and the Revolutionary Movement*, p. 73, see also Gandhi's note on Tolstoy's letter in *M.K. Gandhi: Hind Swaraj and other Writings*, Anthony J. Parel (ed.), p. 136.
3. Ibid., also see Gandhi's role in *M.K. Gandhi: Hind Swaraj and other Writings*, p. 136.
4. M.K. Gandhi, *Collected Works of Mahatma Gandhi*, (referred hereafter as *CWMG*) 1 September to November 1909, vol. IX, p. 303 (Ahmedabad, 1963). This article was sent to the *Indian Opinion* after 16 July 1908, p. 303, document 180.
5. Ibid., p. 480.
6. For Gandhi's commitment to non-violence, see Mark Juergensmeyer 'An Analysis of Gandhi's Political Discourses: Gandhi vs Terrorism' in *Daedalus: Journal of the American Academy of Arts, Sciences*, pp. 113-15, see also Bikhu Parekh, 'Colonization and Reform: An Analysis of Gandhi', *Political Discourse*, pp. 113-71.
7. Gandhi, *CWMG*, April 1911 to March 1913, p. 361.
8. *CWMG*, XLII, October 1929 to February 1930, pp. 341-44.
9. Ibid.

10. Sumit Sarkar, 'The Logic of Gandhian Nationalism: Civil Disobedience Movement and the Gandhi-Irwin Pact, 1930-1931', in *Indian Historical Review*, vol. 3, pp. 114-44.
11. See Appendix III.
12. Nehru, *An Autobiography*, p. 257.
13. Ibid.
14. Robert Bernays, *Naked Faquir*.
15. *The Evolution of India and Pakistan,* C.H. Philips with the cooperation of Dr H.R. Singh and B.N. Pandey, p. 241.
16. CWMG, vol. XLV, December 1930 to April 1931, p. 266 (July 1931).
17. Ibid.
18. Ibid.
19. Ibid., pp. 333-34.
20. The *Tribune*, 28 March 1931.
21. The *Earl of Halifax, Fullness of Days*, p. 149.
22. Ibid., p. 150.
23. Ibid.
24. Nehru to Damodar Swarup, 7 October 1929, in S. Gopal, *Selected Works of Jawaharlal Nehru*, vol. 4, p. 14.
25. Nehru's public speech at Allahabad on 10 March 1931 in *The Leader*, 12 March 1931.
26. *The Trial of Bhagat Singh: Politics of Justice*, A.G. Noorani (ed.) Appendix III, p. 282.
27. Ibid., p. 274.
28. M.M. Juneja (ed.) *Selected Collection on Bhagat Singh*, p. 132.
29. Ibid.
30. Ibid.
31. Aruna Asaf Ali's account in *Great Women of India*, Verinder Grower and Ranjana Arora (ed.) p. 177.
32. Ibid.
33. Madeleine Slade, *The Spirit's Pilgrimage*, p. 124.
34. Robert Bernays, *Naked Faquir*, p. 221.

35. Ibid., p. 221-22.
36. Gandhi to Emerson, 20 March 1931, Home Department. Political, FA/21/1931, p. 31.
37. *CWMG*, March-June, 1930, vol. XLIII, p. 6.
38. S. Gopal, p. 39.
39. Ibid.
40. *O City of Lights: Faiz Ahmad Faiz: Selected Poetry and Biographical Notes*, Translated by David Kamal and Khalid Hasan, Selected and Edited, Khalid Hasan, pp. 60-61.
41. V.N. Datta, 'Nehru and Partition', in *Nehru Revisited*, N. Ram (ed.), pp. 400-1, see also Nehru, *A Bunch of Old Letters*, Bombay, pp. 55-56.
42. *Nehru Revisited*, N. Ram, p. 402.

4

Irwin's Action

On the return of the Conservative Party to power, Stanley Baldwin, the prime minister, appointed Lord Irwin (later Lord Halifax) as the Viceroy of India, a post he held till 1931. Earlier during Andrew Bonar Law's Premiership Irwin had served as the president of the Board of Education (1922-24), and later as the minister of Agriculture and Fisheries (1924-25) during Baldwin's Premiership. Lord Birkenhead, the Secretary of State for India (1924-28), disfavoured Irwin's appointment as the Viceroy. He disliked Irwin's free and progressive views on politics, but Prime Minister Baldwin explained to his opposition that Irwin was the best man for the job, capable enough to meet emergencies. Irwin on his part regarded Baldwin as his political mentor and father figure.

Irwin had family connections with India, being a grandson of Sir Charles Wood (Lord Halifax), who was the president of the Board of Control during Lord Dalhousie's regime. Irwin arrived in Bombay on 1 April 1926 hoping to improve Indo-British relations and calm political tension in the country. Belonging to a distinguished aristocratic family and born with a withered left arm, Irwin, a Fellow of All Souls College, Oxford was a high-minded Tory and a prominent member of the Conservative Party. He was known for his austerity, simplicity of character, and tactical skills. On contentious political issues, he sought the maximum degree of accommodation.[1]

Winston Churchill used the expression 'Holy Fox' for Irwin, implying that Irwin was prudent and a man of sterling character. As Bernays put it:

> Irwin has something more than magnetism. It is a curious spiritual power. He has magnificent head and his bald figure and Cecilian stoop and sympathetic kindly eyes give more the impression of a Prince of Church than of a politican.[2]

Bernays adds: 'He (Irwin) has that rare power possessed by men like Gandhi's fame of making men who meet him spiritually the better for their contact with him.'[3] Harold Macmillan, who became the Prime Minister of Britain later, thought him a 'great gentleman', 'a man of strong religious convictions, and long experience of public life'.[4] After meeting Irwin in Simla in mid-1926, C.F. Andrews noted that Irwin was 'modest and unassuming without the slightest tinge of racial prejudice'.[5] Subhas Chandra Bose thought much of Irwin's sympathetic approach to the solution of India's problems. Bose wrote:

> Though a prominent member of the Conservative Party, he (Irwin) had proved himself a well-wisher of India. After Lord Ripon, no Viceroy had adopted such a friendly attitude

towards the Indian people as he did. That he could not do more was due to the reactionary forces that were working against him in India and England.[6]

S. Gopal too thought that as the Viceroy of India Irwin's approach towards India was constructive and beneficent. As a realist, Irwin understood the rising tides of Indian nationalism, which were animating Indian life and thought. That is why he sought the cooperation of the Indian political parties to resolve India's manifold problems. He believed that however tedious and complex the poltical issues may be, they can be resolved amicably through negotiations and a spirit of mutual trust. He had the additional advantage of conciliating Indian opinion because by 1929 the second Labour minority government headed by Ramsay MacDonald had come into office.

Irwin's Viceroyalty was a period of great political tension. A series of important political issues such as the Simon Commission Report, Nehru Report and the Civil Disobedience movement confronted him. In his statement (known as the Irwin Declaration) he said:

> That he is authorized by His Majesty's government to state clearly that in their judgement it is implicit in the declaration of 1917 that the issue of India's Constitutional progress as therein contemplated is in the attainment of Dominion Status.

The statement also proposed a round table conference between the British government and the representatives of Indian opinion, and to consider the next step after the publication of the Simon Report. Irwin told his party men:

> We have taught (India) the lesson (of Democracy) and she wants us to pay the bill. There is a wind of nationalism and freedom blowing as strongly in Asia as anywhere else in the world.[7]

When the Pact with Gandhi was signed, Baldwin, the leader of the Conservative Party hailed it a 'victory of commonsense, a victory rare enough in India, and rare enough at home'.[8] It has been said that 'few preconsuls other than Irwin could have demonstrated a subtlety of mind to match that of Gandhi and drive so hard a bargain clothed in the language of friendship'.[9] On the eve of the Gandhi-Irwin Pact, the *Statesman* wrote that 'this (Pact) will be regarded as one of the greatest happenings of the second quarter of the twentieth century and possibly as decisive for the world as November 11, 1918'.[10] Initially Gandhi found Irwin 'stiff and rigid', but as their talks proceeded the atmosphere became congenial. For the first time the head of the British government in India talked freely with an Indian leader without any reservation. Imbued with a high sense of purpose, Irwin succeeded in inspiring confidence among the political parties.

The Home government appreciated Irwin's Pact with Gandhi. The Secretary of State William Wedgwood Benn, in his letter dated 6 March 1931 conveyed to Irwin 'a message of grateful thanks and heartiest congratulations on behalf of 180 members of the Parliament for his magnificent and successful efforts to bring peace, prosperity, concord and happiness to the people of India and Britian'.[11] Summing up Irwin's achievement in India, Benn wrote to Irwin on 2 April 1931, 'That you should have been in India (which was Godsend to me) was, I am convinced, a crowning mercy for the Commonwelath.'[12] As noted in the previous Chapter, Irwin had told Gandhi that he held Bhagat Singh guilty of murder and that he found no justification on any ground for the commutation of his death sentence. Irwin was working under certain constraints which prevented him from revoking Bhagat Singh's death sentence, even if he had wanted to do so.

In the execution of his policy in India the Viceroy did not have a free hand nor did any Viceroy. The Viceroy was accountable to the Secretary of State and the Home government. Because of telegraphic communications the Viceroy and the Secretary of State held mutual consultations on crucial political matters.[13] Though Baldwin supported Irwin, there were some influential members of the Conservative Party such as Lord Birkenhead, Lord Salisbury, Douglas Hogg, Alfred Knox, Brandam Bracken, George Lloyd, Winston Churchill, Beaverbrook and a few others who disapproved Irwin's release of Gandhi from jail. They condemned the Gandhi-Irwin Pact as 'disastrous'. They said openly that by 'Irwin's gullibility and overconfidence, India was being given away.'[14]

Due to the onset of the Great Depression, the minority Labour government fell from power, and as a coalition the National government was constituted with Ramsay MacDonald as Prime Minister of which the Conservatives were strong partners. The Viceroy's negotiations with Gandhi infuriated Winston Churchill. About a week before the Gandhi-Irwin Pact in a speech at the West Essex Association on 23 February 1931, he let out a steam of memorable invective.

> It is alarming and nauseating to see Mr Gandhi a seditious Middle Temple lawyer now posing as a *faquir* of a well-known type in the East striding half-naked upon the Viceroy's palace while he is still organizing and conducting a definite campaign of civil disobedience to parley on equal terms with the representative of the King-Emperor.[15]

Churchill did not mince words, and straightway wrote a letter to Irwin expressing his anguish and displeasure on his performance in India. He wrote on 24 March 1931:

> I feel the deepest sorrow at the course of events in India and the impulsion you have given to them. We should be locked in this country for several years. I think that it will be the dividing line in England.[16]

The stiff-necked red-faced blimp British bureaucracy in India was hostile to the idea of conceding anything to the Congress after its confrontation with the Civil Disobedience agitation. About a decade earlier E.S. Montagu, the Secretary of State, visiting India had felt that the Government of India was 'too wooden, too iron, too inelastic, too antediluvian, illogical and indefensible'.[17] Since then things did not change. The British civil servants in India generally approved General Dyer's massacre at Jallianwala Bagh on 13 April 1919. Despite the Adjutant General's warning, they contributed a substantial sum of nearly nine thousand pounds as a mark of tribute to his action with the words 'To the man who saved India'.[18] The relations between the British civil servants and Indians were soured by racial antagonism, mutual distrust, and bitter memories of the past. The Punjab government had a long tradition of ruthless governance which was nourished by Sir John Lawrence, and sustained by Sri Denzil Ibbetson and Michael O'Dwyer. Ibbetson had arrested Lala Lajpat Rai and Ajit Singh and dispatched them to Mandalay. O'Dwyer is known for his Martial Law atrocities, and his defence of Dyer.

Gandhi was very keen on instituting an enquiry into the alleged atrocities committed on people by the police during the Civil Disobedience movement, and he urged the Viceroy to take immediate steps in the matter. There was a lot of pressure put on Gandhi by his colleagues to insist on holding an enquiry into the police excesses. But the Viceroy resisted Gandhi's demand on various grounds. At one stage it seemed as though the Gandhi-Irwin talks were going to break down. The Secretary of State, William Wedgwood Benn, was informed that the Gandhi-Irwin talks had reached a deadlook on the police enquiry issue. In his letter to the Viceroy, dated 21 February 1931, Benn set down some guiding principles for the police conduct which he transmitted to Irwin, while giving him complete discretion to deal with the problem according to the nature of each case. Benn wrote to Irwin:

> You must be guided by your judgement and it is essential that we should be able to establish in the eyes of the world our determination to uphold the highest standard of police's conduct.[19]

Discussions continued for two, three days between Gandhi and Irwin on the police enquiry but without success. Irwin told Gandhi that police enquiry, if conducted, would lead to mutual recriminations and spoil the atmosphere of goodwill and trust which had been created. Irwin then used his wit and tactical skills to win over Gandhi to his point of view. Irwin wrote in his memoirs:

> Everybody would produce evidence in support of what they were setting out to prove; there would be no conceivable means of testing its accuracy; and all that we should achieve would be to exacerbate tempers on both sides. This did not satisfy him at all, and we argued the point for two or three days. Finally, I said that I would tell him the main reason why I could not give him what he wanted. I had no guarantee that he might not start civil disobedience again, and if and when he did, I wanted the police to have their tails up and not down. Whereupon his face lit up and he said, 'Ah, now Your Excellency treats me like General Smuts treated me in South Africa. You do not deny that I have an equitable claim, but you advance unanswerable reasons from the point of view of Government why you cannot meet it. I drop the demand.'[20]

Gandhi was thus persuaded to drop the police enquiry. It seems that Irwin was not telling Gandhi the real difficulties that lay in turning down his request. Robert Bernays who closely watched the Gandhi-Irwin talks tells a different story. He states that Irwin resisted Gandhi's plea because, 'Sir Fredrick Sykes, "a strong man", the Governor of Bombay, and seven other Governors threatened to resign if police enquiry was granted.'[21] Such a threat would defang any Viceroy! About Irwin's rejection of Gandhi's appeal for the commutation of Bhagat Singh's death sentence, Bernays offers a valid explanation as to why Irwin could not commute Bhagat Singh's death sentence.

Bernays wrote:

> It was an extremely difficult situation for the Viceroy. The mention of Bhagat Singh might have driven India back into disorder. The consequences of that at the moment were incalculable for it was on the eve of Karachi Congress. Yet how could he let him (Bhagat Singh) off. *He might well have been faced with the resignation of every head of the police force. So at one stroke the Viceroy had to solve the problem.*[22]

The *People* in its editorial entitled 'The Shadow of Bhagat Singh' dated 22 March 1931 supports Robert Bernays' view that the British civil servants in Punjab had put strong pressure on Irwin not to commute Bhagat Singh's death sentence. The paper wrote:

> Perhaps it goes without saying that some Punjab officials were pressing Lord Irwin to let the condemned be executed. It is said some police officials even threatened to resign if the sentences were commuted. We fail to understand the reasonableness of such an attitude. The condemned persons undoubtedly stand convicted of having murdered two policemen. But, if they are saved from the gallows, nobody would say they got off very cheap. *Add up the sentences of imprisonment awarded in this case, and the total would be in the neighbourhood of two hundred years (if the death sentences are changed into those of life imprisonment).* You don't call that cheap! And the police does function in countries where the penal system rules out the capital sentence.

> Though we do not understand the *reasonableness* of this attitude ascribed to Punjab officials, the *reason* thereof is easy to see. They are perhaps the very people who have all along fought against peace. They are wroth with Lord Irwin. They want neither him nor his peace. Their counsels were ignored and the truce concluded. Defeated but refusing to take their defeat as something final they are busy still with their machinations that would discredit the peace endeavour. If Lord Irwin, on the other hand, still believes in peace, he must know what difficulties he has thrown Mr Gandhi by his rejection of the petitions for mercy. He would be faced at Karachi with opposition from the extreme wing in any case.[23] (Gandhi was going to the Karachi Congress to ratify the Gandhi-Irwin Pact)

G.D. Birla, who knew Irwin personally, highlights the limited authority of a Viceroy which restricts him from acting independently. Citing an example of Lord Linlithgow, who felt utterly helpless, Birla wrote:

> But whenever he (the Viceroy) decides to take a bold action, he will have to face opposition from his own men. I dare say that Lord Halifax (Lord Irwin), had the same experience when he invited Gandhiji to talks.[24]

I have outlined what seem to me the causes for Gandhi not saving Bhagat Singh's life from the gallows. It would be difficult, and probably unnecessary to weigh their relative importance for they interacted upon one another so as to form a single whole. The role of each of these important agencies was dependent on the weight of the imperial control operating in India and England.

As argued above, despite his disapproval of Bhagat Singh's action and constrained as he was by his commitment to non-violence, Gandhi did whatever he could to persuade the Viceroy to commute Bhagat Singh's death sentence. Gandhi's appeal to Irwin was on humanitarian grounds. The decision to commute Bhagat Singh's death sentence lay not in Gandhi's hands but in Irwin's. Irwin took on himself the responsibility for Bhagat's death sentence. He realised, much to his chagrin, how the top-ranking British officials were targeted for assassination. On 17 December 1928, Saunders, a young British police officer was shot dead. Two bombs were thrown in the Central Assembly hall, Delhi on 8 April 1929. A bomb was thrown at the dining room of his own Viceregal train of white carriages outside the Delhi railway station when Irwin was approaching New Delhi on the morning of 23 December 1929. Sir Geoffrey de Montmorency, Governor of Punjab, was shot, and he received injuries at the hands of a young man named Harikrishan at the close of the Convocation in Punjab University on 23 December 1929. In such circumstances, it is doubtful if Irwin, unfettered by external factors, would have commuted the death sentence.

Bhagat Singh had killed a British police officer, and the punishment for murder was hanging. In imperial calculations Bhagat Singh was a cold-blooded butcher who had committed the murder of a fellow human being. From the British perspective, he was a rebel, a seditionist, a challenger, and wrecker of their system, which they were determined zealously to guard against anarchists like him. Irwin realised that the British life in India was unsafe so long as political militancy was not crushed. Of course, he could not ignore the strong feelings of British bureaucracy in India, and of the Home government.

Notes

1. For a candid appraisal of Irwin's character and his political astuteness, see Roy Jenkins, *A Liberal Viceroy* in *Nine Men of Power*, pp. 125-42.
2. Robert Bernays, *Naked Faquir*, p. 51.
3. Ibid., p. 146.
4. Harold Macmillan, *Winds of Change (1914-1939)*, pp. 539-40.
5. Hugh Tinker, *The Ordeal of Love: C.F. Andrews*, p. 220.
6. Subhas Chandra Bose, *The Indian Struggle*, p. 216.
7. Harold Macmillan, *Winds of Change*, p. 270.
8. Dr K. Veerathappa, *British Conservative Party and Indian Independence* (1930-37), p. 48.
9. Parshotam Mehra, *A Dictionary of Modern Indian History* (1907-1947), p. 148.
10. Gopal, op.cit., p. 116.
11. *National Archives of India*, Acc. no. 3890 OR Mss. Eur c 153/II Halifax Collection, January 1930 to April 1931, Telegram from Secretary of State, Wedgwood Benn to Irwin, 6 March 1931, no. 770.
12. Halifax Collection, June 1930 to April 1931, Telegram from Benn to Irwin, Acc. no. 3885, no. 63, p. 394.
13. Roy Jenkins, *Nine Men of Power*, p. 140.
14. Col. G.R. Lane Fox to Irwin, 4 March 1931, Halifax Collection, vol. III, January 1930 to April 31, no. 246.
15. Cited in Andrew Roberts, p. 40.
16. Winston Churchill to Irwin, 24 March 1931, Halifax Collection, vol. III, no. 277.

17. V.N. Datta, *Jallianwala Bagh* p. 30.
18. Nigel Collet, *The Butcher of Amritsar: General Reginald Dyer* p. 206, see also Datta, pp. 150-51
19. Benn to Irwin, 21 February 1931, *Halifax papers* (June 1930 to April 1931), Acc. no. 3890, no. 739.
20. Irwin, *Fullness of Days*, p. 149.
21. Ibid., p. 222.
22. Bernays, p. 222.
23. The *People*, Lahore, 22 March 1931.
24. Birla, p. 192.

5

The Trial

In his study of Bhagat Singh's trial, A.G. Noorani has shown that Bhagat Singh's trial was a farce, politically motivated, and the procedures adopted in his prosecution were devious and a 'negation of justice'.[1] Noorani wrote:

> But, the issue is the fairness of the trial; the sense of fairness of those who staged it—the police, the prosecution, the Magistrate and the three judges on the Tribunal. This was the first case of its kind ever in which twelve persons were tried, convicted and sentenced to death, transportation for life and long terms of imprisonment, for the gravest offences known to law, after a trial which was conducted in their absence.
>
> It was a trial, moreover, by a Special Tribunal set up by the Viceroy's edict in an Ordinance, without recourse to the Central Legislature.[2]

Bhagat Singh was implicated in two cases: the Central Assembly Case, and the Lahore Conspiracy Case. Bhagat Singh and Batukeshwar Dutt were sitting in the visitors' gallery and watching the proceedings of Central Assembly on 8 April 1929. The Public Safety Bill and the Trade Disputes Bill had been passed despite a strong opposition of a majority of members of the Assembly. The Viceroys' Proclamation enacting the Bills was to be formulated. The President of the Assembly, Vithalbhai Patel was expected to give his ruling on the Bills, when two bombs were thrown into the Assembly hall. The bombs exploded, and six persons were slightly injured, including Sir Bomanji Dalal, Sir George Schuster, S.N. Ray, R.R. Rau and Rai Bahadur A.P. Dube. The wooden floor was shattered, the ceiling was hit, and the furniture destroyed.[3]

Dressed in a khaki shirt and khaki shorts, Bhagat Singh had hurled the bombs into the hall, and B.K. Dutt scattered the leaflets, bearing the caption 'The Hindustan Socialist Republican Army'. They shouted the slogans '*Inquilab Zindabad!*' (Long Live the Revolution), and 'Down with Imperialism'. The Viceroy Irwin informed the Secretary of State, Wedgwood Benn about the bomb outrage on 8 April 1929 in his telegram (no 13200).

Reference our telegram no 1309-S, dated 6 April:

> House resumed consideration of Trade Disputes Bill this morning. It was understood that on conclusion of Bill President would give his ruling. Immediately after President announced result of division on Bill and was apparently about to pronounce his ruling, a man in the public gallery threw two bombs with deliberation among the official benches. No one appears to have been seriously injured,

except perhaps Sir Bomanji Dalal, who was struck by a fragment of a bomb. House broke up in confusion and subsequently President adjourned it till Thursday morning. Two men in gallery have been arrested.[4]

Later, the same day Irwin sent another telegram to the Secretary of State:

The two men arrested are Bhagat Singh of Lahore, believed to be an absconder wanted by police and Battakeshwar Dutt, a Bengalee; the two bombs are said to have been thrown by Bhagat Singh. The first landed near the front Government benches, the second among the back Government benches. After throwing the bombs, Bhagat Singh fired two shots from an automatic pistol which then jammed. Both men then threw revolutionary leaflets into the Chamber, asserting this action was taken as a result of provocative action of Government in thrusting on country repressive measures such as Public Safety and Trade Disputes Bills and making indiscriminate arrests of labour leaders. The two men made no attempt to escape or to offer resistance on their arrest.

Sir Bomanji Dalal was wounded in thigh and is in hospital. Sir George Schuster and two other officials were slightly injured. It is remarkable that bomb did not do more serious harm, for the seats were badly damaged and the neighbouring walls and even the ceiling of Chamber damaged.[5]

Sir Sobha Singh, the Honorary Magistrate, Delhi, was sitting in the Public Gallery. As a prosecution witness (no 7) he said that he had sent two policemen to arrest Bhagat Singh and B.K. Dutt.[6] But there was no question of their trying to escape. They surrendered to Sergeant H.D. Terry. Bhagat Singh and B.K. Dutt were produced for trial before the Additional District Magistrate, F.B. Pool in the District Jail, Lahore on 7 May 1929. Asaf Ali, the eminent lawyer, appeared for the defence. Charges were framed, and a regular trial before the Sessions Court Judge Leonard Middleton began in the first week of June 1929. Throughout the court proceedings, Bhagat Singh and B.K. Dutt adopted 'an exemplary attitude', and followed the proceedings of the court with 'intelligent interest'.[7]

Initially, Bhagat Singh was not interested in making any statement in court, but finally he and B.K. Dutt made a statement on 6 June 1929 which Asaf Ali read out. Asaf Ali claimed later that the statement was Bhagat Singh's but he polished only its language.[8] This statement is widely quoted in the studies on Bhagat Singh, and we need not reproduce it.[9] From Bhagat Singh's point of view this statement is important because it explains why the bombs were thrown in the Assembly hall. In their statement, Bhagat Singh and B.K. Dutt assured the government that their intention was not to kill or harm any one but to give a 'friendly warning' to them to understand the rising political aspirations of the Indian people. Their sole purpose was:

> ...to make the deaf hear and to give the heedless timely warning. Others have as keenly felt as we have done, and from under the seeming stillness of the sea of Indian humanity, a veritable storm is about to break out. We have only hoisted this 'danger signal' to warn those who are speeding along

without heeding the grave dangers ahead. We have only marked the end of an era of utopian non-violence, of whose futility the rising generation has been convinced beyond the shadow of doubt.[10]

In the concluding part of their statement Bhagat Singh and B.K. Dutt unfolded their plan of building a Socialist society, liberated from economic exploitation. They explained that their ultimate goal was to establish 'the sovereignty of the proletariat' and a 'world federalism', free from 'the bondage of capitalists and misery of Imperial wars'.[11] The statement warned that in case the present system continued then:

A grim struggle will ensure involving the overthrow of all obstacles, and the establishment of the dictatorship of the proletariat to pave the way for the consummation of the ideal of revolution. Revolution is an inalienable right of mankind. Freedom is an imperishable birthright of all. Labour is the real substance of society. The sovereignty of the people is the ultimate destiny of the worker.[12]

Calling for the denunciation of British Imperialism, the statement championed the cause of equality and liberty for which the existing system of distribution of wealth and the established form of government had to be changed through revolutionary means.

Bhagat Singh's statement is so elegantly and lucidly written that it compels our admiration. The language is cadenced, the narrative compact, and sentences short. Due to the sobriety and seriousness of its theme, the statement takes the form of an essay, which reflects the breadth of outlook and loftiness of thought. Asaf Ali tells us that he had 'polished' Bhagat Singh's language. But it seems that Jawaharlal Nehru gave the finishing touches to Bhagat Singh's statement. Nehru was interested in the well-being of Bhagat Singh. He had also established his reputation as a versatile journalist by the end of the 1920s. Bhagat Singh's statement possessed a distinct literary flavour and wide-ranging historical interest, which were the striking features of Nehru's own prose writings.

Under the provisions of Section 71 of the Indian Penal Code, the Sessions Court sentenced Bhagat Singh and B.K. Dutt to transportation for life on 12 June 1929, which the High Court upheld by rejecting the appeal of the accused. The High Court delivered the judgement on 13 January 1930.

Due to their wide police network, the British authorities found the clues to Saunders' murder, which came to be known as the Lahore Conspiracy Case. The authorities identified twenty-four persons as culprits in the murder case—six of them had absconded and two discharged under various sections. Fifteen were put on trial, and seven others had turned approvers. Of the approvers, Hans Raj Vohra and Jai Gopal gave valuable information to the prosecution for unfolding the entire plan of killing Saunders.

The proceedings of the Lahore Conspiracy Case began on 10 July 1929 in the Court of the Special Magistrate, Rai Sahib Pandit Sri Kishen in Central Jail, Lahore. The first issue to be settled was whether a *prima facie* case existed against the accused. Bhagat Singh showed complete indifference to the proceedings of the case. In the Assembly Bomb Case, Asaf Ali had acted as Bhagat Singh's legal counsel, but not in the Lahore

Conspiracy Case, which seemed to A.G. Noorani a 'mystery'.[13]

The issue is why no eminent lawyer defended Bhagat Singh and his associates in Lahore Conspiracy Case. In Lahore where Bhagat Singh was tried, lawyers like Mukand Lal Puri, Pandit Nanak Chand, Barrister, Dewan Chaman Lall and Mehr Chand Mahajan were available who could openly defend him but none took up his case. But some lawyers did challenge the Viceroy's setting up of a Tribunal for the trial of the accused. Possibly Bhagat Singh did not wish to be defended. He knew what lay in store for him. The lawyers wished to keep themselves out of a British police officer's murder case because they thought that as Bhagat Singh's counsel they might incur the ire of British bureaucracy and judiciary from which they were accustomed to seeking favours. The Congress leaders were in prison due to the Civil Disobedience movement, but still they could manage some legal support, which they did not. Bhagat Singh did engage Lala Duni Chand, a Congress leader and a senior member of the High Court Bar, but that was just in name; he was required only to deal with routine matters. Subhas Chandra Bose had no reservations in expressing his sympathy for Bhagat Singh. He watched the proceedings of the case for three hours with Baba Gurdit Singh of Komagata Maru fame. He was greeted in the court with slogans 'Long Live the Revolution' and 'Down with Imperialism'.[14]

The enquiry before the special magistrate had continued for nine months. Two hundred and thirty witnesses had been examined out of six hundred and twenty-seven. The government felt that the obstructive attitude of the accused had hampered the normal working of the court. Hence, it was thought necessary to take drastic steps to speed up the case. By invoking the special authority vested in him by Section 72 of the Government of India Act (1919), the Viceroy constituted a Tribunal on 1 May 1930 with three High Court judges—J. Coldstream, Agha Haider and G.C. Hilton—to deal with the Lahore Conspiracy Case. Section 72 was as follows:

> The Governor-General may in cases of emergency make and promulgate ordinances for the peace and good government of British India or any part thereof, and any ordinance so made shall for the space of not more than six months from its promulgation, have the like force of law as an Act passed by the Indian legislature; but the power of making ordinance under this section is subject to the like restrictions, as the power of the Indian legislature to make laws; and any ordinance made under this section is subject to the like disallowance as an Act passed by the Indian legislature and may be controlled or superseded by any such Act.

The Tribunal commenced its proceedings on 5 May 1930 in the Poonch House, Lahore. Bhagat Singh refused to be represented by any counsel. He watched the plodding routine of the judiciary with contempt. By his defiance of non-cooperation with the court, he challenged the legitimacy and *locus standi* of the British judicial system as operating in India. Later, Bhagat Singh and his associates decided not to attend the court proceedings despite the pressure put on them by the government to do so. Bhagat Singh and his associates were physically beaten, kicked, lifted, and thrown down. Thorns were pushed into their rectum, and kicks were given to their testicles, but they bore these tortures boldly.[15] They kept up their spirits, knowing well the fate that awaited them. Their refrain was, 'Down with Imperialism', 'Long Live the Revolution' and '*Bharat na reh sakega hargaz ghulam khain*' (India no longer will remain a slave country).

A week after the commencement of the case, a disorderly scene occurred in the court when Bhagat Singh and his comrades were handcuffed, and treated harshly by the police. Seeing the police high-handedness, Justice Agha Haider made the following statement dated 12 May 1931:

> I was not a party to the order of the removal of the accused from the Jail and I was not responsible for it in any way. I disassociate myself from all that took place today in consequence of that order.[16]

Under the Ordinance III of 1930 a Special Tribunal of Justice G.C. Hilton, Sir Abdul Qadir and J.K. Tapp was reconstituted, which started its proceedings on 23 June 1930. The promulgation of the Ordinance disabled Bhagat Singh and his associates from appealing to the High Court. The first prosecution witness G.T. Hamilton Harding, Senior Superintendent of Police, had filed a complaint against Bhagat Singh's involvement in the Lahore Conspiracy Case.[17] The Tribunal awarded death sentences to Bhagat Singh, Raj Guru and Sukhdev on 7 October 1931. Some of the salient points of the judgement were as follows:

1. The Tribunal held Raj Guru guilty of killing Saunders as he fired the first shot that had brought down Saunders under his motorcycle.[18] According to the Tribunal, Raj Guru was

a skilled marksman who had been specially brought from Lahore for the purpose of shooting a British police officer. The Tribunal regarded Sukhdev as the 'brain of the conspiracy with Bhagat Singh as its right arm'.[19] According to the Tribunal, Sukhdev planned and directed the entire conspiracy that led to Saunders' murder. The Tribunal used the word 'ubiquitous' for Bhagat Singh, who coordinated the activities of the revolutionaries located in various places through his frantic efforts. The Tribunal emphasised the value of the gun expert, Mr Churchill's evidence which proved that the empties recovered on 17 December 1929 (when Saunders was murdered) had been fired from the same pistol recovered from Bhagat Singh in the Assembly hall on 8 April 1929 (where he had thrown two bombs).[20] In their judgment, the tribunal commended the literary attainments and the intellectual qualities' of the approver Hans Raj Vohra.

After the prosecution completed its work without cross-examining the defence witnesses, Bhagat Singh's father Sardar Kishan Singh appealed for leave to the Privy Council on behalf of the convicted on 20 September 1930. The issue was whether the Governor General by virtue of the authority vested in him by Section 72 of the 1935 Act could promulgate Ordinance III of 1931 and set up a Special Tribunal with extraordinary powers under the cases of emergency and for the peace and good governance of India.[21] The petitions challenged the Governor General's authority.

Due to the pressure of Lala Duni Chand and Dr Gopichand Bhargava, a petition was filed in the Privy Council contesting the legality of Ordinance III of 1931, which was dismissed on 11 February 1931, and rejected with a detailed note on 27 February 1931. In his telegram to the Viceroy dated 14 February 1931, Pandit Madan Mohan Malaviya appealed for the commutation of Bhagat Singh's death sentence. He wrote:

> I do so not only because I am opposed on grounds of humanity to infliction of death sentence upon a fellow man but also because the execution of these young men whose action was prompted not by any personal or selfish considerations but by patriotic impulses, however misguided, will give shock to public feelings. Such an act of mercy on your Excellency's part will at this juncture produce a beneficial effect on public opinion while the purpose of law and state will be fully met by a sentence of transporation for life.[22]

Jiwan Lal Kapur, who later became the Judge of the Supreme Court, Baljit Singh and Sham Lal sent a telegram to the Viceroy on 16 February 1931 challenging the legality of Bhagat Singh's death warrant since the court that had issued it had ceased to exist after completing its six months tenure on 31 October 1931. The Viceroy rejected the plea. The same group of lawyers filed another habeas corpus appeal which was dismissed by Justice M.V. Bhide on 25 February. Rai Bahadur Badri Nath requested the High Court for leave to the Privy Council against Justice Bhide's order of 25 February. The same day he put in another habeas corpus petition on the ground that Justice Bhide had taken cognisance of the commutation of the sentences, but not the execution of death warrants.[23] Both the petitions, one for leave to appeal to the Privy Council, and the other of habeas corpus were dismissed by the court on 23 March at 3 pm. The government was determined to go ahead with the execution of the convicted, which is evident from the following telegram the Viceroy sent to the Secretary of State on 17 March 1931.

> The Government of India accept the view of the local government that the advantage lies not in waiting after the Karachi session but they consider execution should be carried out not later than 23 March.[24]

Notes

1. A.G. Noorani, *The Trial of Bhagat Singh: Politics of Justice*, pp. 27-216.
2. Ibid., p. 186.
3. *History of Freedom Movement Papers, Lahore Conspiracy Case 1929, Trial of Bhagat Singh*, File no. 6/3 A 16, pp. 18, 24, 30 (National Archives of India).
4. Home Department (Political), 1929, Government of India, File no. 192.
5. Ibid.
6. *History of Freedom Movement Papers*, op.cit., pp. 6, 9.
7. Ibid., p. 31.
8. Noorani, op.cit., p. 33.
9. K.C. Yadav and Babar Singh, *The Fragrance of Freedom*, pp. 247-54.
10. D.N. Gupta, *Bhagat Singh: Selected Speeches and Writings*, p. 20.
11. Ibid., p. 23.

12. Ibid., p. 24.
13. Noorani, op.cit., p. 53.
14. Ibid., p. 103.
15. *Trial of Crown vs Bhagat Singh and Bhatukeshwar Datta*, Acc. no. 26, p. 41.
16. *Trial of Crown vs Bhagat Singh*, Acc. no. 26, p. 6.
17. Home Department, 1931, File no. 4/2/933, p.
18. Ibid.
19. Ibid.
20. Ibid.
21. Malwinder Jit Singh Waraich, *Bhagat Singh: The Eternal Rebel*, p. 156.
22. Madan Mohan Malaviya to the Viceroy in Home Department (1931), op.cit., p. 4.
23. Waraich, pp. 162-63.
24. The Viceroy to Secretary of State, in Home Department, (Political), 1931, File no. 4/12/1931, p. 56.

6

Karachi Congress

Gandhi postponed his departure to attend the Congress session at Karachi for a day in Delhi because he did not want to miss the opportunity of meeting the Viceroy, to discuss with him the question of the commutation of Bhagat Singh and his comrades' death sentence. In his letter to the Viceroy dated 23 March, which he had sent to him by a special messenger, he had suggested that in case his presence was needed for the discussion of Bhagat Singh's commutation of death sentence, he would come. But the Viceroy did not respond to his letter. Gandhi left for Karachi via Lahore to attend the Congress session. His foremost anxiety then was the ratification of his Pact with Irwin.

When Gandhi learnt about the execution of Bhagat Singh, Raj Guru and Sukhdev, he issued, on 23 March, a statement in which he paid tribute to their memory but condemned their use of violent means.[1] He warned the youth of the country against following their example and added:

> We should not utilize our energy, our spirit of sacrifice, our labours and our indomitable courage in the way they have utilized theirs. The country must not be liberated through bloodshed.[2]

In his statement Gandhi criticised the government for 'disregarding the public opinion' and 'missing a golden opportunity to win over the rebels on its side'. He feared that the government by its ruthless action 'had dealt a severe blow to the settlement' (Gandhi-Irwin Pact). Of course, he emphasised that the commutation of the death sentence of these young men 'was not a part of the truce'.[3]

In his statements on Bhagat Singh before he was hanged, Gandhi was reserved, but after his execution, he was forthright and outspoken. In his interview to the Press on 26 March, he stressed that to follow violence would be suicidal 'in this country of self-suppression and timidity bordering on cowardice, we can't have too much sacrifice'.[4] When asked whether the executions would alter his views about the Gandhi-Irwin Pact, he replied, 'I must confess that the staying of these executions was not part of the Pact.'[5]

The news of the execution of Bhagat Singh and his comrades caused widespread resentment throughout the country especially in Punjab, and inflamed strong public opinion against Gandhi for not saving Bhagat Singh and his comrades' lives. Jawaharlal Nehru wrote in his *Autobiography*:

On the very eve of the Congress, a new element of resentment had crept in—the execution of Bhagat Singh. This feeling was especially marked in North India and Karachi, being itself in the North, had attracted a large number of people from the Punjab.[6]

Anticipating that Gandhi might face a protest demonstration in Karachi, he was taken to Malir station, twenty miles from Karachi, but there too as he got off the train, a number of people including young men holding black flags yelled and shouted slogans 'Go back Gandhi' and 'Down with Gandhism'.[7] Calling him the 'ally of the British exploiters in India', they handed to him a bunch of black cloth flowers representing the 'ashes of the patriots'.[8] Robert Bernays, who was present at the Congress session in Karachi wrote: 'an Indian carrying a flag rushed at him (Gandhi) and struck his head with a flag pole'.[9] Munshi Premchand, the novelist, foresaw the difficulties that lay in Gandhi's way at Karachi, and expressed his uneasiness over it in his letter addressed to Dayanarain Nigam of *Zamana*.

> The idea was to go to Karachi, but the execution of Bhagat Singh crushed me. With what hope can I go now? Gandhi will be sniggered at there, the Congress will pass into the hands of irresponsible, rebellious, rabble-rousing sections and there is no place for us there...the future looks utterly dark.[10]

Pattabhi Sitaramayya, the official historian of the Congress, wrote about the tense atmosphere prevailing at the Karachi Congress as follows:

The Karachi Congress which should have met under the radiance of universal joy met really under the gloom cast by the news of the execution of the three youths, Bhagat Singh, Raj Guru and Sukh Dev. The ghosts of these three departed young men were casting a shadow over the assembly. It is no exaggeration to say that at that moment Bhagat Singh's name was as widely known all over India and was as popular as Gandhi's. Gandhi, in spite of his best efforts, had not been able to get the sentences of these three youths commuted. That was not all. They who were praising Gandhi for his strenuous efforts to save their lives began to pour forth volleys of wrath over the language to be adopted in regard to the resolution to be moved for the three martyrs.[11]

Before the condolence resolution on Bhagat Singh and his comrades was taken up at the Karachi session, Gandhi delivered a long speech in which he reaffirmed his faith in non-violence which he regarded as the only right course to follow for the liberation of the country from foreign rule.[12] Gandhi said:

> This with the most High as witness I want to proclaim truth that the way of violence cannot bring *Swaraj*; it can only lead to disaster.[13]

In his speech Gandhi challenged the youth who followed a different path of violence for the attainment of their goal.[14] He exhorted the youth to 'trust his forty years experience of the practice of non-violence' and warned them that 'if they will not, they might kill me but they cannot kill Gandhism. If Truth can be killed then Gandhism can be killed. If non-violence can be killed, Gandhism can be killed.'[15] What is *Gandhism*? he asked! And answered that it 'was nothing but winning *Swaraj* by means of truth and non-violence'.[16] In his speech Gandhi also reiterated that he did not make the commutation of the death sentence of Bhagat Singh and his comrades a part of his Pact with the Viceroy because the Congress Working Committee had not authorised it. He assured his critics that he did his best to save the lives of the patriots.[17] He observed:

> I pleaded with the Viceroy as best as I could. I brought all the pressure at my command to bear on him. I poured my soul into it but no avail.[18]

After condolences were offered on the death of Pandit Motilal Nehru, Maulana Mohammad Ali, Maulavi Mazhar-ul Haq and others at the Karachi Congress, the resolution on the execution of Bhagat Singh and his comrades was taken as the first item on the agenda for discussion. The resolution read as follows:

> This Congress, while dissociating itself from and disapproving of political violence in any shape or form, places on record its admiration of the bravery and sacrifice of the late Bhagat Singh and his comrades Syts. Sukh Dev and Raj Guru, and mourns with the bereaved families the loss of these lives. The Congress is of opinion that this triple execution is an act of wanton vengeance and is a deliberate flouting of the unanimous demand of the Nation of commutation. This Congress is further of opinion that Government have lost the golden opportunity of promoting goodwill between the two nations, admittedly held to be essential at this juncture, and of winning over to the method of peace the party which, being driven to despair, resorts to political violence.[19]

While moving the resolution at the Karachi Congress, Jawaharlal Nehru lauded the patriotic spirit and sacrifice of Bhagat Singh, Raj Guru, and Sukhdev. He acknowledged that by their fiery patriotism and courage, the three young men had aroused national consciousness from one end of the country to another.[20] He mentioned specifically the courage and heroism of Bhagat Singh, 'a legendary hero', who gave a 'clean fight' and 'faced his enemy in open field'.[21] But like Gandhi, Nehru too warned the country against following the Bhagat Singh way as that would surely ruin the country.[22] He said, 'We have always rejected violent means and we shall continue to do so.' And the only way, he thought, to win freedom, was 'the noblest way of non-violence', which Gandhi had taught.

Some Congress members suggested a few amendments to the resolution on Bhagat Singh and his comrades. They objected to the opening sentence, which read, 'The Congress, while disassociating itself from and disapproving of political violence in any shape or form'. There was an uproar at the meeting but despite some opposition from Jamnadass Mehta, Sardulsingh Caveesher and Abdul Ghaffar Khan, the resolution was carried.[23]

Addressing the Congress delegates, again Gandhi exhorted them not to 'imitate' Bhagat Singh and his associates by using violent means. He said:

> I am not prepared to believe that the country has benefited from their action. I can only see the harm that has been done. We could have won *Swaraj* long ago if that line of action had not been pursued and we could have waged a purely non-violent struggle. However, no one can deny the

fact that if the practice of seeking justice through murders is established amongst us, we shall start murdering one another for what we believe to be justice.[24]

...Hence, though we praise the courage of these brave men, we should never countenance their activities.[25]

The British Intelligence Report dated 7 April 1931 gives an inside story of the Karachi Congress.[26] It shows how Gandhi with his brilliant strategical skills had succeeded in rallying a large support for the ratification of his Pact with the Viceroy. At one point he threatened that he would go into retirement if no Pact was signed.[27] He knew that Jawaharlal Nehru, Subhas Chandra Bose and other left-wing dissidents were opposed to his truce with the Viceroy. The execution of Bhagat Singh and his associates had placed him in a tight spot because he had failed to save their lives. According to the Intelligence Report, the first step that Gandhi took was to placate the extremists by sponsoring a resolution, which advocated the release of all political prisoners, violent or otherwise. Further, he asked Nehru to move the resolution on the Gandhi-Irwin Pact. The Report also points out that Gandhi had secured from business magnets including G.D. Birla Rs 18 lakhs with promises of 30 lakhs for the Congress delegation, which was going to attend the forthcoming Round Table Conference in London. There is also a short account in the Report on Gandhi's parleys with Subhas Chandra Bose whom he won over to his point of view by assuring him that in case the British government refused to take concrete steps for India's constitutional advancement to self-government, then he would not hesitate in launching a 'war' on British Imperialism. He also ensured the presence of Bhagat Singh's father Kishan Singh to mollify his critics, who were accusing him of not saving Bhagat Singh from the gallows.

According to the Intelligence Report, Gandhi came out floating a 'grandiose document' which he had prepared with the assistance of Nehru to satisfy the left-wing radical groups within the Congress that was aspiring to build up a Socialist form of society in the country.[28] Moving the resolution on Fundamental Rights and Economic Policy at the Congress session, Gandhi highlighted some of their striking features such as Socialist nationalisation of key industries and services, and other measures to reduce the burden of the poor and neutrality in religious matters.[29]

It is clear from the above account that at the Karachi Congress Gandhi had his own way. The Gandhi-Irwin Pact was ratified and the resolution on Bhagat Singh and his associates was passed according to Gandhi's wishes. The Intelligence Report regarded his performance at the Karachi Congress a *tour de force* because he converted his defeat 'in the Civil Disobedience movement' into victory.[30] Nehru wrote in his *Autobiography*, 'The Karachi Congress was an ever great personal triumph for Gandhiji than any previous Congress had been.... It was the Mahatma who dominated the scene.'[31] Munshi Premchand heaved a sigh of relief when Gandhi's views prevailed at the Karachi Congress.[32] He was anxious lest the Gandhi-Irwin Pact was rejected. Premchand hailed the Gandhi-Irwin Pact a triumph of moral force over brute force. It is clear from Gandhi's role at the Karachi Congress that his views on Bhagat Singh and his action remained consistent, which is confirmed by the following letter dated 26 June 1931 addressed to Mehta Anand Kishore, General Secretary of the All India Bhagat Singh, Raj Guru, Sukh Dev Memorial Society.

> I have your letter of the 13th instant. A memorial erected in honour of anybody undoubtedly means that the memorialists would copy the deeds of those in whose memory they erect the memorial. It is also an invitation to posterity to copy such deeds. I am therefore unable to identify myself in any way with the memorial.[33]

This letter from Mehta Anand Kishore to Gandhi was intercepted by the C.I.D. Director. Anand Kishore had appealed to Gandhi for raising funds to build a memorial in honour of the three martyrs, who had died for the country.

Notes

1. *CWMG*, vol. XLV (1930-31), p. 335.
2. Ibid., p. 336
3. Ibid.
4. Ibid., p. 344
5. Ibid., p. 345.
6. Nehru, *An Autobiography*, p. 265.
7. *CWMG*, op.cit., p. 348.
8. Ibid., p. 347.
9. Robert Bernays, *Naked Faquir*, p. 235.
10. Geetanjali Pandey, *Between Two Worlds: An Intellectual Biography of Premchand*, p. 52.
11. Pattabhi Sitaramayya, *The History of the Indian National Congress, (1885-1935)*, vol. I, p. 456.
12. *CWMG*, op.cit., pp. 347-439.

13. Ibid., p. 352.
14. Ibid., pp. 349-50.
15. Ibid.
16. Ibid., p. 350.
17. Ibid.
18. Ibid., p. 351.
19. Sitaramayya, pp. 456-57.
20. *Selected Works of Jawaharlal Nehru*, S. Gopal (ed.), vol. iv (1973), p. 505.
21. Ibid.
22. Ibid.
23. Home Department (1931), File no. 136, p. 14.
24. *CWMG*, op.cit., p. 360.
25. Ibid.
26. Home Department of op.cit., see especially Appendix to the Report addressed to H.W. Emerson.
27. Ibid., pp. 13-14.
28. Ibid., p. 31.
29. Appendix IV, Karachi Congress Resolution, see also, *CWMG*, op.cit., pp. 272-74.
30. Home Department (1931), File no. 4.12.31.
31. Nehru, *An Autobiography*, p. 265.
32. Geetanjali Pandey, p. 73.
33. *Gandhi to Mehta Anand Kishore, 20 June 1931*, in Home Department (Political, 1931), File no. 4, pp. 12-31, p. 7.

7

Conclusion

It has been argued in this work that despite his firm commitment to non-violence, which remained a cardinal principle of his life, Gandhi put the maximum pressure on the Viceroy Lord Irwin for the commutation of the death sentence of Bhagat Singh and his comrades, who were found guilty of committing the murder of a senior British police officer. Gandhi disapproved their action. In this study, Gandhi's attitude to Bhagat Singh and his associates' death sentence has been examined against the background of his negotiations with the Viceroy for the settlement of outstanding political issues facing the country. Irwin had established a rapport with Gandhi, and held him in high esteem for his integrity of character. Gandhi too respected Irwin for his candour and goodwill. Despite a general view prevalent in historical studies on Bhagat Singh that Gandhi and Irwin could on their own commute Bhagat Singh's death sentence, this study shows that the issue of saving his and his comrades' lives lay beyond Irwin and Gandhi, because they were not free and independent enough to do whatever they wished as is commonly assumed. They had to act within the framework of the British Imperial system operating in the country.

Gandhi condemned violent acts. His soul rebelled against them. When it came to the adoption of violent means by an individual or political party, he refused to countenance. That is why he called Bhagat Singh a 'misguided youth', who, he thought, had done immense harm to the cause of India's struggle for independence. Both on moral and pragmatic grounds, Gandhi denounced Bhagat Singh and his comrades' action. Gandhi's critics have argued that he could have made the commutation of Bhagat Singh and his comrades' death sentence a condition for signing the Gandhi-Irwin Pact. But how could he do so since such a course would have been contrary to his own ethics and also to the policy of the Congress? Hence there was no question of his terminating his truce with the Viceroy, nor could he undertake a fast unto death for compelling the government to reduce Bhagat Singh's death sentence to life imprisonment. Possibly he could have rallied a wide public support for the abolition of capital punishment in principle. Capital punishment is still prevalent in China, the US, Britain and India. Of course, for certain heinous crimes, capital punishment is necessary but Bhagat Singh's act does not seem to fall in this category. Why did Gandhi not plead for the abolition of capital punishment in principle for all the criminals? In that case possibly Bhagat Singh and his comrades might have been sentenced to life imprisonment till they were freed on the dawn of India's independence on 15 August 1947.

Some historians and writers are of the view that Bhagat Singh was a staunch Marxist. Sohan Singh Josh, who was closely associated with Bhagat Singh, emphasised that Bhagat Singh was a full-fledged Communist who was committed to the 'orthodox ideals' of Marxism. In a recent article entitled 'Bhagat Singh: Profile and Legacy of a Revolutionary', K.N. Panikkar presents Bhagat Singh as one of the early Marxists and Leninites, who 'embraced a revolutionary movement' informed by Marxism.[1] In his Foreword to the book *Bhagat Singh: Select Speeches and Writings* edited by D.N. Gupta, Bipan Chandra calls Bhagat Singh a revolutionary and a Marxist in the making, and adds that 'he was not so much what he became but what he was capable of becoming'.[2] Ajoy Ghosh, who became the general secretary of the Communist Party, later stressed that during the last phase of his life, Bhagat Singh's interest in Socialism grew; but it would be an exaggeration to say that Bhagat Singh was a Marxist, though he had begun to feel the necessity of taking armed action individually and collectively against the British government in India.

In the writings of left-wing historians, Bhagat Singh is represented as wearing a Marxian garb. This work emphasises that being a sensitive and highly intelligent youth, Bhagat Singh had become deeply interested in Marxism after the suspension of the Non-Cooperation movement, which was the last phase of his life. But before that period there were potentially strong multiple influences that had worked on him and influenced his thinking, such as, the Arya Samaj, the Ghadrites, and the Babbar Akalis. There were also his personal contacts with some notable personalities who had moulded his political outlook and acted as an impulse to his actions. Belonging to the family of Arya Samajists and revolutionaries, Bhagat Singh was at heart a Ghadrite with strong leanings towards Marxism. Bhagat Singh's religion was liberty, his slogan was *Inquilab Zindabad*, and his goal was Socialism.

Bhagat Singh wrote his essay entitled 'Why I am an Atheist?' in the Central Jail, Lahore, before he was executed on 23 March 1931. The essay was handed over to his father Sardar Kishan Singh after his execution. It was published on 31 September 1931 in the *People*, which had been established by Lala Lajpat Rai and Lala Feroz Chand. The essay has high literary merits. It shows historical insight and mature thinking. It is terse, compact, and elegantly written. Bhagat Singh had published a number of articles in the *Kirti* and *Chand*. It is natural that his articles were edited, when published in newspapers and journals.

As noted earlier, Bhagat Singh had a disrupted education. He could not complete his school education. He moved from one place to another. It is true that he read voraciously during his prison days. Statements issued by him in the court were amended by Asaf Ali, which is understandable. Of course, he had access to the Dwarkadas Library from where he obtained books on various subjects for his self-study. It raises doubts how a person of his disrupted educational background could at the age of twenty-three or so write such commendable literary and scholarly pieces reflecting a maturity of thought, a wide sweep of history, and a mastery of the English language. The original documents including his letters are not available. The authorship of the articles attributed to him still remains a mystery.

It has been argued by several writers, including the late Danial Latifi, a well-known senior advocate, that there was a secret understanding between Gandhi and Irwin that Bhagat Singh would be reprieved after the Pact was ratified by the Congress at its session in Karachi. But the secret was disclosed by a member of the Congress Working Committee which infuriated the British bureaucracy making it difficult for the Viceroy to commute the death sentence. Danial Latifi observes:

> There is probability in the story that this Reviewer heard that there was a secret understanding between Mahatma Gandhi and the Viceroy that Bhagat Singh would be reprieved (if circumstances permitted) after the Pact was ratified and the public euphoria thereby generated gave the Viceroy elbow room to commute the death sentence. The premature leakage of the news of this understanding by a Congress Working Committee member and the public's triumphant reaction made this secret understanding infructuous in a manner that left no option to the Viceroy but to proceed with the execution and to Gandhiji to keep quiet—since Congress men had violated the understanding.[3]

For long this writer too believed in the story of this secret agreement between Gandhi and Irwin on saving Bhagat Singh's life. But in the light of Irwin's own autobiography, *Fullness of Days*, the story of the secret deal appears to be a canard.

Irwin (later Lord Halifax) was a man of sterling character, a devout Christian highly respected for his integrity. He gave up the prime ministership in favour of Winston Churchill on the eve of the Second World War because he thought that

Churchill was the right man to lead the nation in war. He played a constructive role for the independence of India in early 1947 when his own Conservative Party led by Churchill was obstructing it. In his memoir Lord Halifax makes no mention of his deal with Gandhi on Bhagat Singh's death sentence. Robert Bernays, the most reliable witness to the Gandhi-Irwin talks, too makes no such mention of any deal between Irwin and Gandhi on Bhagat Singh's death sentence. This settles the question.

Whether or not Bhagat Singh would have accepted a commutation of his death sentence is a different matter. Bhim Sen Sachar, then a noted Congress worker, met Bhagat Singh in the condemned cell of Lahore Central Jail in 1930. Sachar suggested to Bhagat Singh to opt for a commutation of his death sentence so that he could serve the country to which Bhagat Singh replied, 'No, the country will be served better by my sacrifice.'[4]

In his illuminating article, 'The Ideological Development of the Revolutionary Terrorists in Northern India in the 1920s', Bipan Chandra explained how Bhagat Singh and his co-workers, despite their dedication and single-mindedness had failed to realise their objects.[5] According to him, Bhagat Singh and his comrades, the young and spirited, and ever anxious to produce quick results were urban-based, and did not care to mobilise masses for consolidating their fighting strength to wage a united struggle against British power. Bhagat Singh and his associates were too confident to be prudent. They were in a hurry to do things. They were dashing, bold, and patriotic but lacked political leadership and financial resources to coordinate their activities. They did not realise their own limitations nor the strength of their adversary and had neither the support of the bourgeoisie or the masses. They failed to gain moral ascendancy because the country and political parties were unwilling to accept their methods.

What kind of image did the public have of Bhagat Singh? How was he viewed? What did people think of him? Of course Bhagat Singh and his comrades thought that they were doing the right thing for the country. They believed that only violent means in India's struggle for freedom could cripple British authority in India. They stood their ground, and held their beliefs firmly. Nothing could break their spirit or stifle their enthusiasm. They were men of courage and honour. Various influences, that worked on them, historical and personal, convinced them that a non-violent struggle for the promotion of self-rule would fail.

Gandhi thought that Bhagat Singh was a 'misguided youth', who had gone wrong. The British considered Bhagat Singh a rebel and a criminal, who must be hanged. The liberals, who advanced India's cause of self-government through constitutional means, reproached him for his disorderly conduct. The hunger strike undertaken by Bhagat Singh and his comrades in jail had aroused widespread sympathy for them in the country. When they were charged with the crime of Saunders' murder, they began to be perceived by the public as freedom fighters who were dying for the love of their country. When they were executed, the nation turned them into 'martyrs', to be lauded, revered, and honoured. In his *Autobiography*, Nehru wrote:

> Bhagat Singh became a symbol, the act was forgotten, the symbol remained and within a few months each town and village of Punjab and to a lesser extent in the rest of north India resounded with his name. Innumerable songs grew up about him and the popularity that the man achieved was amazing.[6]

As discussed in the last chapter, the resolutions on the Fundamental Rights and Economic Policy passed by the Karachi Congress were the offshoots of the constitution of the Hindustan Republican Association. The Congress adopted the slogan '*Inquilab Zindabad!*' which became the battle-cry for the youth of the country. This slogan was loudly raised at political forums, even though the meaning of the word '*Inquilab*' was seldom understood by those attending such meetings.

Nehru was absolutely right when he wrote movingly that Bhagat Singh became a symbol and remained so. Yes, a symbol he remained, just a name to be conjured with, a name to be remembered, and paid tributes on his birth and death anniversary ritualistically. In our national historiography he is barely mentioned, and generally relegated to a footnote; and treated, of course, as an outsider, a deviant, and a maverick, and not a valiant co-partner in the mainstream of the Indian freedom movement. Such are the turns and twists of history!

The tragedy of Bhagat Singh and his comrades was not that they were idealists in the path of the deterministic *juggernaut* represented by the British Imperial system, but their schemes and programmes might have been realised had the Congress and other political parties, and the country, not chosen other paths. They were as much the victims of Congress politics as of the British Imperial system. This writer has reasons to believe that though Bhagat Singh had challenged the Gandhian political morality, Gandhi, despite his disapproval of Bhagat Singh's action, regarded his sacrifice a patriotic one, and Gandhi would not mind many Bhagat Singhs dying for the freedom of the country and sacrificing themselves. Didn't the Mahatma too sacrifice all he had for the country? A sacrifice never goes in vain! There is a great lesson to be learnt from 'constructive destruction'. A flower must die to yield its place to the fruit, and flower must perish for the seeds to sprout again. The cycle of history carries on.

Notes

1. K.N. Panikkar in *Frontline*, vol. 24, no. 21, pp. 6-7, 12, 2 November 2007, New Delhi.
2. D.N. Gupta, op.cit., vii-viii.
3. Danial Latifi, 'Birtish Justice on Trial', reproduced from some material published in the January issue of *Indian Book Chronicle* and republished in *Indian Book Chronicle*, Jaipur, March 2006, p. 11.
4. G.S. Bhargava, *Bhim Sen Sachar: An Intimate Biography*, New Delhi, 1997, p. 34
5. Bipan Chandra, 'The Ideological Development of the Revolutionary Terrorists in Northern India in the 1920s', in *Socialism in India*, B.R. Nanda (ed.), pp. 163-89
6. Nehru, *An Autobiography*, pp. 175-76.

8

Recollections

The following account relating to Bhagat Singh and his execution was given to this writer by Mr Pratap Singh[1], now eighty-seven, originally a resident of Amritsar, but at present living at 511, New Friends Colony, New Delhi.

Born in 1920, Pratap Singh was educated in the Hindu Sabha School, and the Hindu Sabha College, Amristar, where he took his BA. A bright student and widely read in Marxist literature, he started working for the Communist Party. His father Gurdit Singh owned a well-known gramophone shop 'S. Uttam Singh and Sons' in Hall Bazar, Amritsar. Gurdit Singh was the President of the Amristar District Naujawan Bharat Sabha. Pratap Singh was about eleven years old when

---

1. Mr Pratap Singh's account is based on the interview, which this writer had with him at the India International Centre, New Delhi, on 28 October 2007.

Bhagat Singh was executed. He recalls that when Bhagat Singh was on the run after killing Saunders, he stayed for four days at his father's residence in Hall Bazar. He also remembers that after his execution, Bhagat Singh and his comrades' popularity and reputation reached sky-high, whereas Gandhi and the Congress were severely criticised for not saving Bhagat Singh's life.

Pratap Singh also maintains that a general view prevailed that the Viceroy Irwin had agreed to Gandhi's proposal of reducing Bhagat Singh's death sentence to life imprisonment, but Dr Muhammad Alam, a member of the Congress Working Committee, who knew of this secret deal, divulged it to his confidants. Knowing the Viceroy's design of reducing the death sentence, the British civil servants threatened to resign. At this, the Viceroy had to resile, and order Bhagat Singh's execution.

*

Mrs Pushpa Datta (*nee* Pushpa Bakshi), now ninety, belonged to a well-known Bakshi family of Lahore, and lived at Dev Samaj Road, Lahore, before the Partition of India in 1947. Her father Bakshi Raghunath Sahai was a Professor of Botany, and her uncle Bakshi Ram Rattan, the Principal of D.V. College, Lahore. After the Partition of India, Pushpa migrated to Jaipur and settled there. As she is related to me, I meet her when she visits Delhi.

At Pushpa's residence at Lahore, this writer used to meet the members of Vohra family, including Hans Raj Vohra (who had turned an approver in Bhagat Singh's murder case), his mother; his wife, Tara; and his sister, Raj. Recollecting her close associations with the Vohra family, Pushpa gave to this writer the following information:

1. Hans Raj Vohra's father Guranditta Mal Vohra had put a great pressure on his son to become a government approver. Pushpa also said that a close family-friend or a relation, an ICS officer, holding a high position in the judicial service, had persuaded Hans Raj Vohra to reveal the conspiracy about killing Saunders, which he did. According to Pushpa, it was Hans Raj Vohra's mother who confided to her this information.
2. Pushpa also recalled that after Hans Raj had turned an approver, the Vohra family became a target of public censure and condemned as traitorous. This tirade and maligning was a nerve-racking experience for the family, which became shattered, and developed abnormal traits in their behaviour. Some members developed a tendency to go into hysterics.

A secret Intelligence Home Department, Government of India file (no 25/65/1930) throws light on how Hans Raj Vohra's father Guranditta Mal Vohra, the Principal of Central College, Lahore, managed through the Punjab Governor, and the Viceroy to send away his son to England after he had turned an approver. Guranditta Mal Vohra thought it absolutely necessary to 'get him (his son) out of India as his life was in danger in India'. Hans Raj Vohra sailed to England by the ship *Rampura* on 15 November 1930. Guranditta Mal Vohra had wanted his son to be admitted to Cambridge University for his studies. The Viceroy Irwin advised Guranditta Mal Vohra to contact the Deputy High Commissioner in India for the admission of his son to an educational institution in England. Hans Raj Vohra had no hand in killing Saunders, but he was fully cognisant of the entire conspiracy to kill him. His evidence in Bhagat Singh's trial proved crucial for the benefit of the government.

Hans Raj Vohra took to journalism in England. On return to India he joined the British Tory paper *The Civil and Military Gazette*, Lahore. Later he served in the *Statesman*, Calcutta, and then shifted to the US where he worked as a special correspondent of the *Times of India* until he died there.

Appendices

APPENDIX – I

Beware, Ye Bureaucracy: Notice of Hindustan Socialist Republican Association (Army)

J.P. Saunders is dead; Lala Lajpat Rai is avenged

Really it is horrible to imagine that so lowly and violent hand of an ordinary Police Official, J.P. Saunders could ever dare to touch in such an insulting way the body of one so old, so revered and so loved by 300 million people of Hindustan and thus cause his death. The youth and manhood of India was challenged by blows hurled down on the head of India's nationhood. And let the world know that India still lives; that the blood of youth has not been totally cooled down and that they can still risk their lives, if the honour of their nation is at stake. And it is proved through this act by those obscure who are ever persecuted, condemned and denounced even by their own people.

'Beware, Ye Tyrants; Beware'

Do not injure the feelings of a downtrodden and oppressed country. Think twice before perpetrating such diabolical deed. And remember that despite 'Arms Act' and strict guards against the smuggling of arms, the revolvers will ever continue to flow in—if not sufficient at present for an armed revolt, then at least sufficient to avenge the national insults. In spite of all the denunciations and condemnation of their own kiths and kins, and ruthless repression and persecution of the alien government, party of young men will ever live to teach a lesson to the haughty rulers. They will be so bold as to cry even amidst the raging storm of opposition and repression, even on the scaffold.

'Long Live the Revolution'

Sorry for the death of a man. But in this man has died the representative of an institution which is so cruel, lowly and so base that it must be abolished. In this man has died an agent of the British authority in India—the most tyrannical of Govt. of Govts. in the world.

Sorry for the bloodshed of a human being; but the sacrifice of individuals at the altar of the Revolution that will bring freedom to all and make the exploitation of man by man impossible, is inevitable.

Long Live the Revolution!

Balraj*
Commander-in Chief

Dated 18 December 1928

---

*'Balraj' was the pseudonym of Chandra Shekhar Azad, the Commander-in-Chief of the Hindustan Socialist Republican Association (Army).

APPENDIX – II

To Make the Deaf Hear: Notice of Hindustan Socialist Republican Association

'It takes a loud voice to make the deaf hear.' With these immortal words uttered on a similar occasion by Valliant, a French anarchist martyr, do we strongly justify this action of ours.

Without repeating the humiliating history of the past ten years of the working of the reforms and without mentioning the insults hurled down on the head of the Indian nation through this House, the so-called Indian Parliament, we see that this time again, while the people expecting some more crumbs of reforms from the Simon Commission, are ever quarrelling over the distribution of the expected bones, the Govt. is thrusting upon us new repressive measures like those of the Public Safety and Trade Disputes Bill, while reserving the Press Sedition Bill for the next session. The indiscriminate arrests of labour leaders working in the open field clearly indicate whither the wind blows.

In these extremely provocative circumstances, the Hindustan Socialist Republican Association, in all seriousness, realizing the full responsibility, had decided and ordered its army to do this particular action, so that a stop be put to this humiliating farce and to let the alien bureaucratic exploiters do what they wish, but to make them come before the public eye in their naked form.

Let the representatives of the people return to their constituencies and prepare the masses for the coming revolution. And let the Government know that, while protesting against the Public Safety and Trade Disputes Bills and the callous murder of Lala Lajpat Rai on behalf of the helpless Indian masses, we want to emphasise the lesson often repeated by history that it is easy to kill individuals but you cannot kill the ideas. Great empires crumbled but the ideas survived. Bourbons and Czars fell while the revolution marched ahead triumphantly.

We are sorry to admit that we who attach so great a sanctity to human life, who dream of a glorious future, when man will be enjoying perfect peace and full liberty, have been forced to shed human blood. But the sacrifice of individuals at the altar of the great revolution that will bring freedom to all, rendering the exploitation of man by man impossible, is inevitable.

Long Live the Revolution!

Balraj
Commander-in-Chief

APPENDIX – III

The following statement by the Governor-General in Council is published for general information:-

1. Consequent on the conversations that have taken place between His Excellency the Viceroy and Mr. Gandhi, it has been arranged that the civil disobedience movement be discontinued, and that, with the approval of His Majesty's

Government, certain action be taken by the Government of India and local Government.

2. As regards constitutional questions, the scope of future discussion is stated, with the assent of His Majesty's Government, to be with the object of considering further the scheme for the constitutional Government of India discussed at the Round Table Conference. Of the scheme there outlined, Federation is an essential part; so also are Indian responsibility and reservations or safeguards in the interests of India, for such matters as, for instance, defence; external affairs; the position of minorities; the financial credit of India, and the discharge of obligations.

3. In pursuance of the statement made by the Prime Minister in his announcement of the 19th of January 1931, steps will be taken for the participation of the representatives of the Congress in the further discussions that are to take place on the scheme of constitutional reform.

4. The settlement relates to activities directly connected with the civil disobedience movement.

5. Civil disobedience will be effectively discontinued and reciprocal action will be taken by Government. The effective discontinuance of the civil disobedience movement means the effective discontinuance of all activities in furtherance thereof, by whatever methods pursued and, in particular, the following:

   (1) The organized defiance of the provisions of any law.
   (2) The movement for the non-repayment of land revenue and other legal dues.

(3) The publication of news-sheets in support of the civil disobedience movement.
   (4) Attempts to influence civil and military servants or village officials against Government or to persuade them to resign their posts.
6. As regard the boycott of foreign goods, there are two issues involved, firstly, the character of the boycott and secondly, the methods employed in giving effect to it. The position of Government is as follows. They approve of the encouragement of Indian industries as part of the economic and industrial movement designed to improve the material conditions of India, and they have no desire to discourage methods of propaganda, persuasion or advertisement pursued with this object in view, which do not interfere with the freedom of action of individuals, or are not prejudicial to the maintenance of law and order. But the boycott on non-Indian goods (except of cloth which has been applied to all foreign cloth) has been directed during the civil disobedience movement chiefly, if not exclusively, against British goods, and in regard to these it has been admittedly employed in order to exert pressure for political ends.
7. It is accepted that a boycott of this character, and organized for this purpose, will not be consistent with the participation of representatives of the Congress in a frank and friendly discussion of constitutional questions between representatives of British India, of the Indian States, and of His Majesty's Government and poltical parties in England, which the settlement is intended to secure. It is, therefore, agreed that

the discontinuance of the civil disobedience movement connotes the definite discontinuance of the employment of the boycott of British commodities as a political weapon and that, in consequence, those who have given up, during a time of political excitement, the sale or purchase of British goods must be left free without any form of restraint to change their attitude if they so desire....

8. Mr. Gandhi has drawn the attention of Government to specific allegations against the conduct of the police, and represented the desirability of a public enquiry into them. In present circumstances Government see great difficulty in this course and feel that it must inevitably lead to charges and counter-charges, and so militate against the re-establishment of peace. Having regard to these considerations, Mr. Gandhi agreed not to press the matter.[1]

Notes

1. *Select Documents on the History of India and Pakistan, IV, the Evolution of India and Pakistan (1858-1947)*, C.H. Philips and Dr B.N. Pandey (ed.) 1962, pp. 241-42.

APPENDIX – IV

Resolution on Fundamental Rights and Economic Changes

31 March 1931

This Congress is of opinion that to enable the masses to appreciate what swaraj, as conceived by the Congress, will mean to them, it is desirable to state the position of the Congress in a manner easily understood by them. In order to end the exploitation of the masses, political freedom must include real economic freedom of the starving millions. The Congress, therefore, declare that any constitution which may be agreed to on its behalf should provide, or enable the Swaraj Government to provide, for the following:

1. Fundamental rights of the people, including

   (a) freedom of association and combination;
   (b) freedom of speech and of the Press;
   (c) freedom of conscience and the free profession and practice of religion, subject to public order and morality;
   (d) protection of the culture, language and scripts of the minorities;
   (e) equal rights and obligations of all citizens, without any bar on account of sex;
   (f) no disability to attach to any citizen by reason of his or her religion, caste or creed or sex in regard to public

employment, office of power or honour and in the exercise of any trade or calling;
(g) equal rights to all citizens in regard to public roads, wells, schools and other places of public resort;
(h) right to keep and bear arms in accordance with regulations and reservations made in that behalf;
(i) no person shall be deprived of his liberty nor shall his dwelling or property be entered, sequestered or confiscated save in accordance with law.

2. Religious neutrality on the part of the State.
3. Adult suffrage.
4. Free primary education.
5. A living wage for industrial workers, limited hours of labour, healthy conditions of work, protection against the economic consequences of old age, sickness and unemployment.
6. Labour to be freed from serfdom or conditions bordering on serfdom.
7. Protection of women workers, and specially adequate provisions for leave during maternity period.
8. Prohibition against employment of children of school-going age in factories.
9. Rights of labour to form unions to protect their interests with suitable machinery for settlement of disputes by arbitration.
10. Substantial reduction in agricultural rent or revenue paid by the peasantry, and in case of uneconomic holdings exemption from rent for such period as may be necessary,

relief being given to small zamindars wherever necessary by reason of such reduction.
11. Imposition of a progressive income tax on agricultural incomes above a fixed minimum.
12. A graduated inheritance tax.
13. Military expenditure to be reduced by at least one half of the present scale.
14. Expenditure and salaries in civil departments to be largely reduced. No servant of the State, other than specially employed, experts and the like, to be paid above a certain fixed figure which should not exceed Rs. 500 per month.
15. Protection of indigenous cloth by exclusion of foreign cloth and foreign yarn from the country.
16. Total prohibitation of intoxicating drinks and drugs.
17. No duty on salt manufactured in India.
18. Control over exchange and currency policy so as to help Indian industries and bring relief to the masses.
19. Control by the State of key industries and ownership of mineral resources.

Control of usury % direct or indirect.

It shall be open to the A.I.C.C. to revise, amend or add to the foregoing so far as such revision, amendment or addition is not inconsistent with the policy and principles thereof.

A.I.C.C. File no.199,1931. Courtsey: Nehru Memorial Museum and Library.

Bibliography

National Archives of India
1. Halifax Collection, 1831-1928.
2. History of the Freedom Movement: Proceedings in the Lahore Conspiracy Case, *Crown vs Bhagat Singh* and others, Part I & Part II.
3. The Lahore Conspiracy Case: Judgement on the Saunders Murder Case.
4. Proceedings of the Home Department (Political), Government of India, 1928-1930.
5. Proceedings of the Home Department (Judicial), Government of India, 1928-1930.

Nehru Memorial Museum and Library
1. Bhagat Singh Papers.

Other works cited
1. Bernays, Robert, *Naked Faquir* (London, 1931).
2. Bhargava, G.S., *Bhim Sen Sachar: An Intimage Biography* (New Delhi, 1997).
3. Birla, G.D., *In the shadow of the Mahatma* (Bombay, 1968).

4. Bose, Subhas Chandra, *The Indian Struggle* (1920-42) (Calculta, 1964).
5. Brown, Emily C., *Har Dyal, Hindu Revolutionary* (New Delhi 1975).
6. Brown, Judith M., *Gandhi, Prisoner of Hope* (London, 1989).
7. Chandra, Bipan on 'Bhagat Singh' in Ravi Dayal *We Fought Together for Freedom: Chapters from the Indian National Movement* (New Delhi, 1995).
8. 'The Ideological Development of the Revolutionary Terrorists in Northern India in the 1920s', in *Socialism in India*, B.R. Nanda (ed.) (Delhi, 1972).
9. Datta, V.N., *Jallianwala Bagh* (Kurukshetra, 1969).
10. ———, *Madan Lal Dhingra* (New Delhi, 1978).
11. Deol, D.S., *Shaheed Bhagat Singh, A Biography* (New York, 1951).
12. Fisher, Louis, *The Life of Mahatma Gandhi* (New York, 1951).
13. Gandhi, M.K., *Collected Works of Mahatma Gandhi*, vols. IX, XLII and XLV (Ahmedabad, 1963, 1970 and 1971).
14. Pandey, Geetanjali, *Between Two Worlds: An Intellectual Biography of Premchand* (New Delhi, 1989).
15. Gopal, S., *Selected Works of Jawaharlal Nehru*, first series vol. 4 (New Delhi, 1973).
16. ———, *The Viceroyalty of Lord Irwin* (Oxford, 1967).
17. Ghosh, Ajoy, *Bhagat Singh and His Comrades* (Bombay, 1946).
18. Grover, Verinder and Ranjana Arora (eds.), *Great Women of Modern India* (New Delhi, 1993).
19. Gupta, D.N., *Bhagat Singh: Selected Speeches and Writings* (New Delhi, 2007).
20. Gupta, Manmathnath, *Bhagat Singh and His Times* (Delhi, 1977).
21. Habib, S. Irfan, 'To Make the Deaf Hear,' *Ideology and*

Programme of Bhagat Singh and His Comrades: Three Essays, (New Delhi, 2007)
22. Halifax, Earl of, *Fullness of Days* (London, 1957).
23. Jenkins, Roy, *Nine Men of Power* (London, 1974).
24. Jones, Kenneth, *Arya Dharma, Hindu Consciousness in 19th Century Punjab* (New Delhi, 1988).
25. Juneja, M.M. (ed.), *Selected Collection on Bhagat Singh* (Hisaer 2007).
26. Khullar, K.K., *Shaheed Bhagat Singh, A Biography* (New Delhi, 1969).
27. Kumar, Ravinder and Sharma Hari Dev (eds.), *Selected Works of Moti Lal Nehru*, (1929-1931), vol. 7 (New Delhi, 1998).
28. Lal, Chaman, *Ghadar Party Nayak, Kartar Singh Sarabha*, (Hindi) (New Delhi, 2000).
29. Macmillian, Harold, *Winds of Change (1914-1939)* (London 2007).
30. Mehra, Parshotam, *A Dictionary of Modern Indian History* (New Delhi, 1985).
31. Mitrokin, L.V., *Last Days of Bhagat Singh in Lenin in India* (Delhi, 1981).
32. Nayar, Kuldip, *The Martyr Bhagat Singh: Experiments in Revolution* (New Delhi, 2001).
33. ———, *Without Fear: The Life and Trial of Bhagat Singh* (New Delhi, 2007)
34. Moon, Sir Penderal, *The British Conquest and Division of India* (London, 1990).
35. Nehru, Jawaharlal, *An Autobiography* (London, 1936).
36. Noorani, A.G., *The Trial of Bhagat Singh: Politics of Justice* (New Delhi, 1996).
37. O'Dwyer, Sir Michael, *India as I Knew it (1925-1995)* (London, 1925).

38. Parekh, Bhikhu, *Colonization, Traditions and Reforms: An Analysis of Gandhi's Political Discourses* (New Delhi, 1989).
39. Parel, Anthony J., *Hind Swaraj and other Writings* (Cambridge, 1997).
40. Parmanand, *Ap Biti* (Urdu), (Lahore, 1922).
41. Philip, C.H. with the cooperation of Professor H.L. Singh and B.N. Pandey (eds.), *Select Documents on the History of India and Pakistan* (1859-1947), vol. 4 (London, 1962).
42. Puri, Harish, *Ghadar Movement, Ideology, Organization and Strategy* (Amritsar, 1983).
43. Robert, Andrews, *The Holy Fox: A Biography of Lord Halifax* (London, 1991).
44. Sitaramayya, Pattabhi B., *The History of the Indian National Congress* (1885-1935), vol. 1 (Delhi, 1969).
45. Shankar, Girja, *Social Trends in Indian National Movement (A Study of Congress Socialist Party)* (Meerut, 1987).
46. Slade, Madeleine, *The Spirit's Pilgrimage* (London, 1960).
47. Tendulkar, D.G., *Mahatma: Life of Mohan Das Karam Chand Gandhi (1885-1935)*, vol. 1 (Bombay, 1952).
48. Tinker, Hugh, *The Ordeal of Love: CF Andrews* (London, 1979).
49. Veerathapa, K., *British Conservative Party and Indian Independence* (1930-1947) (New Delhi, 1976).
50. Waraich, *Malwinder Jit Singh: Bhagat Singh: The Eternal Rebel* (New Delhi, 2007).
51. Yadav, K.C., Babar Singh (eds.), *Bhagat Singh, A Biography* (Gurgaon, 2007).
52. ———, *The Fragrance of Freedom: Writings of Bhagat Singh* (Gurgaon, 2006).
53. ———, *Making of a Revolutionary: Contemporary Portrayals* (Gurgaon, 2006).

54. ———, *Jail Notes of a Revolutionary* (Gurgaon, 2007).
55. ———, *Jatinder Nath Sanyal: Sardar Bhagat Singh: A Biography* (Gurgaon, 2006).
56. Yadav and Arya K.S. (eds.), *Arya Samaj and the Freedom Movement (1875-1918)* (Gurgaon 1988).

Newspapers and Journals, etc.
The *Tribune*, Lahore, (1928-1931)
The *People*, Lahore, 22 March 1931
The *Mainstream*, New Delhi, 6 April 1996
———, 22 June 1996
———, 27 July 1996
———, 22 March 1997
Kirti, Lahore, March 1928
Mukti, New Delhi, July 1972
Chand, New Delhi, November 1928
The *Leader*, Allahabad, 12 March 1931
Frontline, 2 November 2007
Daedulus, Journal of the American Academy of Arts and Sciences (Cambridge, US), Winter issue, 2007

Index

A.I.C.C., 114
Acquines, Thomas, 23
Alam, Muhammad (Dr), 102
Alexander I, 12
Ali, Aruna Asaf, 47
Ali, Asaf, 46-47, 72, 74, 95
Ali, Mohammad (Maulana), 86
All Parties Conference
  (December 1929), 26
Amristar District Naujawan
  Bharat Sabha, 101
Andrews, C.F., 22, 57, 67
Anwar, Khurshid (Khawaja), 51
Arya Samaj, 15, 19, 20, 21, 24, 94
Assembly Bomb Case, 46, 70,
  74-75
Azad, Chandra Shekhar, 27, 51,
  106

Babbar (lion) Akalis, 19, 94
Bakshi, Raghunath Sahai, 102
Bakshi, Ram Rattan, 102
Bakshi, S.R., 2
Baldwin, Stanley, 56, 59, 60
Balraj, 106, 108
Bande Matram, 51
Basin, Prem, 8-9
Benn, William Wedgwood, 59-60,
  62, 70
Bernays, Robert, 40, 47, 48 63,
  64, 84, 97

Naked Faquir, 40
*Bhagat Singh: Select Speeches
  and Writings*, 94
Bhargava, Gopichand (Dr.), 78
Bhide, M.V. (Justice), 79
Birkenhead (Lord), 56, 60
Birla, G.D., 39, 65, 88
Black Ordinance, 33
Bodin, John, 23
Bolshevik regime, 23
Bose, Rash Bihari, 19
Bose, Subhas Chandra,
  2, 10, 25, 31-32,
  48, 52, 57, 75, 88
Bracken, Brandam, 60
British Intelligence Report, 88
  on Karachi Congress, 88-89
Brown, Emily C., 21
Brown, Judith, 5
Bukharin, Nikolai, 23
Burke, Edmund, 23
Byron, *Prisoner of Chillon*, 23

Caveesher, Sardulsingh, 87
Celly, Ashok, 2
  *Bhagat Singh, Bose and the
  Mahatma*, 2
Chand, 95
Chand, Duni (Lala), 75, 78
Chand, Feroz, 95
Chand, Nanak (Pandit), 75

Chander, Ram, 27
Chandra, Bipan, 94, 97
Chattopadhyaya, Virendranath, 52
Chauri Chaura incident, 25
Chibber, Balmukand, 18
Chirol, Valentine, 24
  India, Old and New, 24
Chittagong Army Case, 51
Christ, Jesus, *Sermon on the Mount*, 34
Churchill, Winston, 40, 57, 60, 78, 96, 97
The Civil and Military Gazette, 104
Civil disobedience movement, 39, 40, 58, 61, 62, 89, 108-111
  calling off, 39-40
Clough, Arthur, 24
Coldstream, J., 76
Colonisation Bills, 16
Congress Working Committee, 11, 86, 96, 102
Conservative Party, 59

Dalal, Bomanji (Sir), 70, 71
Dalal, C.B., 8
  Diary of Mahadev Desai, 8
Dalhousie (Lord), 56
Das, Chhabil, 20
Das, D.P., 4, 7, 8, 49
Das, Jatindranath, 16
Datta, Pushpa (*nee* Pushpa Bakshi), 102
Dyal, Har, 18, 21
de Montmorency, Geoffrey, 66
Defence of India Act, 15
Delhi Conspiracy Case, 18, 29

Deol, D.S., 2-3, 13
Dhingra, Madan Lal, 17, 32, 35, 48
Dhritarashtra, 11
Dostoevsky, Fyodor, 23
  Crime and Punishment, 23
Dube, A.P. (Rai Bahadur), 70
Dussehra bomb outrage, 27
Dutt, Batukeshwar, 16, 28, 70, 72-74
Dyer (General), 46, 61

Emerson, H.W., 49, 50
Emerson, Herbert (Sir), 5
Engels, Fredrich, 23

Faiz, Ahmad Faiz, 51
Fundamental Rights and Economic policy,
  resolution of, 89, 99, 112

Gandhi, Mahatma,
  attitude on Bhagat Singh's execution, 1-12, 31-55, 92
  A Catastrophe, 36-37
  in Karachi, 84
  speech at,
    Congress Nagpur session, 24
    Karachi Congress, 85-86, 87-88
Gandhi-Irwin Pact, 8, 46, 49, 65, 83
Gandhi-Irwin talks, 4
  on Bhagat Singh, 4-5
Gandhism, 85
Ghadar, 18
Ghadr Party, 18, 19, 21

Ghadrites, 18, 19, 21, 94
Ghosh, Ajoy, 94
Gita, 35
Gopal, S., 3, 50, 51, 58
Government of India Act (1919), Section 72, 76
Government of India Act (1935), Section 72, 78
Great Depression, 60
Gupta, D.N., 94
Gupta, Manmathnath, 4, 49
What Gandhi Did and Did Not Do, 4

Habib, Irfan, 9-10
Haider, Agha (Justice), 76, 77
Halifax (Lord), 56, 65, 96
Haq, Mazhar-ul (Maulavi), 86
Hardinge (Lord) (Viceory), 18, 22
Harding, G.T. Hamilton, 77
Harikrishan, 66
Hilton, G.C., 76, 77
Hind Swaraj, 34-35
Hindustan Republican Army, 50
Hindustan Socialist Republican Association (HRSA), 10, 26, 27, 99, 105, 107
Hirachand, Walchand, 39
Hogg, Douglas, 60
Hugo, Victor, *Les Misérables*, 23

Ibbetson, Denzil, 62
INA, 3
Indian Opinion, 32, 34, 36
Indian Penal Code, Section 71, 74

Inquilab Zindabad, 28, 70, 95, 99
Institute of Imperial Studies, London, 32
Intelligence Home Department, 103
Irish revolutionary movement, 20
Irwin (Lord), 3, 4, 13, 25, 31, 38, 40, 56, 116
 Declaration, 58
 autobiography, *Fullness of Days*, 96-97

Jallianwala Bagh massacre, 22, 45-46, 61
Jang, Sher, 51
Jayakar, M.R., 26, 39
Jenkins, Roy, 5
Jinnah, Mohammed Ali, 45, 46
Jinnah's Fourteen Points (March 1928), 26
Johnson, Allan Comphell, 5
Jones, Kenneth, 19
 Arya Dharma, 19
Josh, Sohan Singh, 94

Kakori Dacoity Case, 51
Kapur, Jiwan Lal, 79
Karachi Congress, 3, 10, 65
Kaumi Vidya-pith, 19
Kautsky, Karl, 23
Khan, Abdul Ghaffar, 87
Khayyam, Omar, 23
Khullar, K.K., 3
Kirti, 17, 95
Kishen, Sri (Pandit) (Rai Sahib), 74
Knox, Alfred, 60

Kohat riot, 25
Komagata Maru, 75

Lahore Conspiracy Case, 16, 21, 22, 45, 70, 74, 75, 76, 77, 80, 115
Lal, Sham, 79
Lall, Dewan Chaman, 75
Latifi, Danial, 96
Law, Andrew Bonar, 56
Lawrence, John (Sir), 62
Lenin, 23, 26, 51
Linlithgow (Lord), 65
Lloyd, George, 60
Locke, John, 23

Morley (Lord), 32
MacDonald, Ramsay, 38, 58, 60
Macmillan, Harold, 57
Madras Congress, 52
Mahabharata, 11
Mahajan, Mehr Chand, 75
Mainstream weekly, 4, 6, 7
Malaviya, Madan Mohan (Pandit), 79
Marx, Karl, 23, 26, 51
Meerut Conspiracy Case, 51
Mehta, Anand Kishore, 90
Mehta, Jamnadass, 87
Middleton, Leonard, 72
Mill, J.S., 23
Mira Behn, 47
Montagu, E.S., 61
Moon, Penderel (Sir), 5

Naidu, Sarojani, 47
Napoleon, 11

Nath, Badri (Rai Bahadur), 79
National College, 19-20
Naujawan Bharat Sabha, 26-27, 101
Nauriya, Anil, 7
  Clemency Effort for Bhagat Singh, 9
  The Trial of Bhagat Singh, 7
  The Writing of History, 8
Nayar, Kuldip, 2, 10
  The Martyr, Bhagat Singh: Experiments in Revolution, 10
  Without Fear: The Life and Trial of Bhagat Singh, 10
Nehru Report (1928), 26, 58
Nehru, Jawaharlal, 10, 16, 17, 25, 28, 39, 44, 54, 74, 83, 87, 88, 91, 116
  Autobiography, *India As I Knew It*, 17, 18, 83, 89, 98
Nehru, Motilal, 16-18, 86
News Chronicle, 40, 47
Nigam, Dayanarain, 84
Non-Cooperation movement, 19, 22, 25, 94
Noorani, A.G., 6-9, 69, 75
  Gandhi and Bhagat Singh article, 9
  The Trial of Bhagat Singh, 6

O'Dwyer, Michael (Sir), 18-19, 22, 46, 62
  Martial Law atrocities of, 46, 62
October Revolution of 1917, 23
Ordinance III,
  of 1930, 77
  of 1931, challenged, 78

Paine, Thomas, 23
Panikkar, K.N., 94
  Bhagat Singh: Profile and Legacy of a Revolutionary, 94
Parmanand (Bhai), 18, 19, 22
  Twarikh-I-Hind, 21
Patanjali, *Yoga Sutra*, 37
Patel, Vithalbhai, 70
People, 64, 95
Philips, C.H., 5
Pingley, N.G., 19
Plato, 23
Polak, H.S.L., 34
Pool, F.B., 72
Pratap, 19
Premchand, Munshi, 84, 89
Press Sedition Bill, 107
Privy Council, 78-80
Public Safety Bill, 45, 70, 71, 107, 108
Puri, Mukand Lal, 75

Qadir, Abdul (Sir), 77

Rai, Lala Lajpat
  16, 19, 28, 62, 95, 105, 108
  death of, 28
Raj Guru, 27, 77, 82, 85-87
Rakhi, Ram, 18
Rau, R.R., 70
Ray, S.N., 70
Regulation of 1818, 16
Ripon (Lord), 57
Roberts, Andrew, 5
Round Table Conference, 39, 40, 58, 88, 109

Rousseau, Jean-Jacques, 23, 34
  Social Contract, 34
Russell, Bertrand, 23
Russian Revolution, 18, 20, 23, 51
  effect on Bhagat Singh, 18, 20, 23, 51

Sachar, Bhim Sen, 97
Salisbury, Lord, 60
Sanyal, Jitendra Nath, 22
Sapru, Tej Bahadur (Sir), 8, 26, 39
Sarabha, Kartar Singh, 19, 21, 29, 117
Sarkar, Sumit, 39
Sastri, Srinivasa, 8, 39
Satyagraha movement, 49
Saunders, John Poyantz, murder of, 27, 28, 31, 66, 74, 77, 78, 98, 102-104
Savarkar, V.D., 21, 32
Schuster, George (Sir), 70, 71
Second World War, 96
Simon Commission, 26, 28, 58, 107
  proposals (May 1930), 26
  Report, 58
Simon, John (Sir), 28
Sinclair, Upton,
  Boston 24
  Oil, 24
Sindhu, Virendra, 20
  Yugdrashta Bhagat Singh aur uske Mritunjay Purkha, 20
Singh, Ajit (Sardar), 15-16, 62
Singh, Baljit, 79
Singh, Bhagat,
  arrest of, 27, 72

and Dutt, statement of, 72-74
death sentence to, 77
  issue of commutation, 3, 41-43, 46-47, 49, 50, 53, 66, 79, 82, 92, 93, 97
execution of, 82, 83, 86-88
hanged, 28
hunger strike in jail, 6, 16, 45
hurling bombs at Central Assembly hall, 28, 31, 66, 70
interest in Socialism, 22, 23, 44, 73, 94, 95
self-education of, 15-30
trial of, 69-81
tribute to Dhingra, 17-18
Why I am an Atheist? essay, 95
Singh, Chanan, 27
Singh, Gurdit (Baba), 75, 101
Singh, Kishan (Sardar), 15, 78, 89, 95
Singh, Mohan (General), 3
Singh, Pratap, 101-102
Singh, Sobha (Sir), 71
Sinn Fein Party, 32
Sitaramayya, Pattabhi, 4, 84
Smuts (General), 63
Socialist ideology, 52
Socrates, 23
Spear, Percival, 5
Spinoza, 23
Statesman, 59, 104
Sukh Dev, 28, 77, 78, 82, 87
Swaraj, 51, 85-87, 112
Sykes, Fredrick (Sir), 63

Tagore, Rabindranath, 45

renounciation of Knighthood, 45-46
Tapp, J.K., 77
Tendulkar, D.G., 3
Tennyson, 23
  A Charge of the Light Brigade, 23
  Morte d'Arthur, 23
Terry H.D., 72
Thakurdas, Purshottamdas, 39
Thoreau, 37
Tilsit, 11
Times of India, 104
Tolstoy, 37
Trade Disputes Bill, 45, 70, 71, 107, 108
Transval Asians, 33
Trotsky, Leon, 23

Valliant, 107
Vidyalankar, Jaichandra, 20
Vir Arjun, 26
Vohra, Bhagwati Charan, 27
Vohra, Guranditta Mal, 103
Vohra, Hans Raj, 74, 78, 102, 103, 104

West Essex Association, 60
Wood, Charles (Sir), 56
Wyllie, William Curzon (Sir), 17, 32, 48
  killing of, 32

Young India, 2
Yudhishtira, 11

Zamana, 84